T0146409

KIDNAPPER BY PROXY

DORIS M HOLLAND

authorHOUSE®

AuthorHouse™
1663 Liberty Drive
Bloomington, IN 47403
www.authorhouse.com
Phone: 1 (800) 839-8640

Published by AuthorHouse 03/17/2017

ISBN: 978-1-5246-8382-5 (sc)
ISBN: 978-1-5246-8383-2 (hc)
ISBN: 978-1-5246-8381-8 (e)

Library of Congress Control Number: 2017904029

CONTENTS

CHAPTER 1

KAYLA MEETS SANDY

Kayla heard the sound of little feet coming fast behind her but paid little attention. She was used to hearing the clap, clap, clap, of short quick steps of small children. They had only one speed, fast. That is as fast as their small little legs could carry them. As a teacher of second graders she heard this sound a lot. But this pair of feet was much younger. She could tell because the steps were much shorter.

"*Some mother must be out shopping with her toddler,*" She thought as she smiled at the pleasant sound and walked on to finish her shopping.

"Mommy," Kayla looked down into the face of a wide eyed little girl who had taken hold of her hand. The child looked up at her with a wide smile. "I lost you Mommy when you went to try on that pretty dress. Did you buy it? Let me see." The sandy haired child pulled Kayla's bag out of her hands, set it on the floor, and peered down into it. "It was so pretty on you. But you didn't buy it?" The child looked up with a sad face. "Why?"

"It wasn't appropriate. It was a very expensive dress and much too formal." Kayla answered without thinking. "*Why am I answering this child's questions? This is crazy.*"

Kayla was stunned as she looked around for a mother who must be frantically looking for her child. Seeing no one she stooped down and looked into the child's eyes. "Sweetheart, have you lost your mommy? Why don't we go find her?" she suggested as she took the child's hand and searched for a customer service sign. Before she found one two men in uniform came on each side of her, "Is this your child?" one asked in a demanding voice but low as if not to attract attention.

"Why no," Kayla answered, "She just showed up and took my hand. I was on my way to report to a clerk so she could announce that a child had been found."

"Come with us," she was instructed as the child was carried off in another direction. She had tears streaming down her pink face as she kicked and screamed, "Mommy, Mommy." She pleaded in a heartbreaking cry as she reached out her arms toward Kayla.

Kayla sat up in bed with a jerk, "Thank goodness it was just a dream." Then she looked over at the sandy haired little girl curled up next to her. She looked so peaceful in her sleep. Kayla realized part of it wasn't a dream. This little bundle of sweet innocence had come to her last afternoon and had taken her hand as if it were the most normal thing in the world.

"What happened? How did I end up in this situation? I was in my own world as I looked at a formal dress remembering my childhood dreams.

"It was always the same dream. I would dress up in my aunt's stage costumes and pretend I was going to a fancy ball. We had so much fun as my aunt danced with me. I was just a child but the dream seemed so real. I must have been about ten when I was reprimanded and told to stop with my daydreaming. That I was too old to continue with such make-believe fantasies.

"What's the harm? No one is here to tell me I can't." I told myself. *"I'll just try it on to see how it looks. I have plenty of time. It'll be fun to daydream again.*

"I really liked it but I didn't have anywhere to go to wear something that fancy. I hung it back on the rack and continued shopping. That's when I felt a small hand take hold of mine. She looked up at me with large brown eyes, 'Mommy,' she said with the sweetest innocent smile, 'I lost you.' She wrapped her little arms around my legs and held on as if she was afraid I would disappear. Now here she is asleep in my bed."

"What am I to do with you little one?"

She could still hear the stranger who reprimanded her, "Shame on you! How could you deny this beautiful child? Social services should take her away where you could never get your hands on her."

"No! No! Mommy, don't let them take me. I'll be good." She begged as she wrapped her arms around Kayla's legs and held on tight. "Please Mommy let's go home. I don't like what that mean man said."

That disturbed her now that she had more time to think about it. Why would a child think someone would take her away? Why would she need to promise to be good? Why was there fear in the child's eyes when the mall security guard tried to take her hand to lead her to her office?

"I don't understand why no one came back looking for you." Kayla was puzzled.

The only part of the dream that wasn't real was the authorities taking her to jail. But that could be a possibility if she kept the child. Kayla had stayed in the store well after the mall closed. She tried to assure the child that her mother was looking for her and she would be worried.

"Maybe I just look like her mother," she thought, *"But that isn't reasonable. Children know their own mother."*

She had tried desperately to find the parent or somebody who had brought the child to the mall. But to no avail. She couldn't just walk away and pretend nothing was wrong.

With the child crying and declaring Kayla was her mother what else could she to do? So here she was with a child that wasn't hers sleeping peacefully on her bed.

Danny and Becky watched the scene in the department store. The child had found Kayla and was clinging to her as she had been programmed to do. "It's working. Let's get out of here." They walked casually out the door so as to not call attention to themselves. But it didn't work. As soon as they crossed the door, alarms went off startling the two, "What?"

The sound was still vibrating throughout the store as the security guard walked over, "It seems you have merchandise that hasn't been paid for. Would you come with me, please?"

Danny looked around to see if anyone was watching the scene as they followed the security officer, *"Thank goodness. This probably happens all the time."* No one seemed to be paying much attention.

"What have you done?" He whispered to Becky. His askance glare at her made her bristle.

"Me? What have you done?" she whispered throwing the accusation back at him.

As they entered the office Becky remembered the beaded handbag she had dropped into her oversize purse. She **had** planned to pay for it **this** time. It was an honest mistake. With all the tension they had gone through watching their pigeon she had just forgotten.

"I'm awfully sorry sir. I just forgot about that handbag. I was going to buy it but I plain forgot when **my husband insisted we needed to get home now**." She shot an angry glance at Danny.

"That's perfectly understandable Ma'am. Just wait here for a second I'll see what I can do. I hope you understand there are certain procedures we have to follow." He smiled a placating smile as he left the room.

"You idiot! What have you done now?" Danny whispered with a grinding of his teeth.

"Hey it was your stupid idea that we act like normal shoppers."

The security guard walked over a few isles and used his cell phone. "Hey boss I got a problem here at the store. But it is more down my alley as a police officer than as a security officer here. I may need your help on this one. I think I have a couple of fugitives in my office." He listened for a while and then answered "Okay Boss."

He returned to his office just as the two jumped back as if guilty of something. But Officer Black didn't let on that he noticed. "Okay Mr. and Miss…. Oh I'm sorry I didn't get your names. I'm Officer Dillon Black by the way."

"Bobby Dubois," Danny announced in an arrogant swagger and pointed his thumb at his companion, "and this here's my wife Jean."

"I think we can get this settled now. If you'll follow me I'll go with you to the cashier," Officer Black walked toward the service counter.

"You know Officer after all the racket and embarrassment this store caused I don't think I want the bag now." At that Becky aka Jean handed him the said bag and strutted out.

Officer Black called his boss back, "Okay they left. Now what do we do? Yes sir I'm sure I saw their faces on the wanted board. It may have been some time ago. But you know I never forget a face." He laughed at his own joke.

On the other end of the conversation his boss, Chief White was saying, "We'll let them think the coast is clear while we check files to see what comes up."

CHAPTER 2

MARGE AND RENE'

"It was odd I assure you. The situation was reversed. It's usually a child being kidnapped by an adult not an adult being kidnapped by a child." Marge made the joke to lighten the mood."

The mall security officer Marge Brown and the manager of the upscale boutique, Sophisticates, were discussing the activity that had taken place the day before. Marge had invited Rene' to meet her for coffee at one of the shops in the mall's food court. She wanted to review the case and thought it would be better for Rene' to meet in a less stressful place than in her office. Since no official action had taken place and no paperwork had been filed she was trying to cover her tracks.

Rene' had been shaken by the experience. Her nerves were still on edge "It was very disturbing. I didn't know what to do. The child was crying calling her Mommy and the woman kept insisting she wasn't her mother. The child was so upset and the woman was discretely trying to comfort her while trying to get enough information so she could find the parent. Then a customer overheard the conversation and accosted the woman about her role as a mother. The situation was about to get out of hand. That's why I called you."

"It took a long time to explore the situation and by that time it was late." Marge had quietly gone to every store in the mall and surveyed tapes from the security cameras for a worried parent. But there wasn't anyone that fit the description.

"It took a long time to review the tapes. I didn't want to involve Social Services that late at night especially with a child that small involved. She was already quite attached to the woman who found her. The child was clinging to her and would not let her go. It was heartbreaking to hear the two of them. The child insisting the woman was her mother and the woman in turn insisting that she was not her mother." Marge seemed to be rehearsing the explanation she was sure to be giving her supervisor.

Rene' had worries of her own. "I hope I don't lose my franchise. My company fancies itself as having an aura of stylishly elegance. So I could be in trouble if any negative feedback gets back to headquarters. I just opened this franchise and can't afford to lose it. It was a dream of mine to own my own shop. So I saved up and bought my own boutique. I bought this classy joint and bought into the franchise. I sank all my savings and had to borrow the rest to just get started. I pray the Lord will let me enjoy the pleasure of it for a little while at least." Rene' was rambling and she knew it.

I just I hope I don't lose my job either. I didn't quite go by protocol but I felt so sorry for the child and Kayla."

"I know what you mean. I couldn't help feel for both of them myself," René wiped at a tear that threatened to surface. Her nerves had not yet settled. "We needed a private place to talk so I asked the woman and child to go with me to my office. I didn't call anyone but you."

"I had no way of knowing if Kayla was or was not her mother. So I made my decision to believe the child and let her go home with Kayla based on two scenarios: What I know about emergency child placement and what I found out about Kayla when I ran her name through a background check."

Marge set her cup down and leaned toward René and whispered, "Let's just say I have had occasion to be on the receiving end of child placement cases. I'll just leave it at that."

"What about Kayla?" René was eager to hear what Marge had discovered about her.

"Clean as a whistle. Not even a parking ticket. She teaches second graders and is highly respected by the staff and fellow teachers. We didn't have to question her colleagues. She was selected teacher of the year and her records are open to the public."

"What I don't understand is why the child so adamantly insisted that Kayla was her mother. And Kayla insisted she wasn't," René shrugged her shoulders in question.

Marge reached for the ringing cellphone attached to her belt, "Uh oh, my boss. I'd better take this. Excuse me." She unclipped the phone from her belt and stepped away from the table.

When she returned she had a concerned look on her face, "Here goes nothing. I am being summoned by my boss. Wish me luck."

CHAPTER 3

OLD UGLY

Danny and Becky pulled the ten-year old beat up faded Chevy into a dilapidated apartment complex. After riding around on side roads long enough to determine no one was following them, they decided it was safe to go home. Home was just a place to stay until their next move.

Becky tossed her large purse on the pile of sheets and blankets on the unmade bed scattering the contents and threw herself on the space that was left. As she stretched out on the bed Danny slumped down on the overstuffed chair in the corner. He pulled a pair of Becky's shorts from under him and held them up with his fore finger and thumb then dropped them on the floor. "Do you just drop your clothes where you pull them off?"

There was no response from the bed. She had heard enough of his complaints already. It had been a rough day especially after being caught with the purse and almost arrested.

Danny couldn't sit still. "I need a smoke," he said it to himself as well as to Becky. He got up and went outside. His nerves were on edge after the incident at the boutique. "I'm just hungry. That's what it is. I need something to eat," he told himself as he went back inside. He swiped his face with his palm as he looked at the sink overrun with dirty dishes.

"Don't you ever clean this place? I know it's a dump but a little cleaning would make it look a little better."

"Yep it's a dump alright. Why don't you clean it up? You're here as much as I am."

Becky looked at the open closet. The door barely hanging on a hinge was pressed against a pile of dirty clothes that had spilled into the doorway.

"We should go to the laundry mat but it's too late. Maybe we'll do it tomorrow." She didn't like the potential work she was looking at so she turned over in bed. The sight from there wasn't any better. The pattern on sheer cloth that served as a curtain had faded so that it was no longer recognizable. A big rip in the 'curtain' exposed a bent in the Venetian blind put there by years of peeking out. She flipped over on her stomach and rested her chin on her folded arms. Just thinking about work made her tired. "Anyway it's late and I'm too tired to argue with you. What do we do now? What's the plan?"

"We can't do much of anything now. With that stunt you pulled at the store we'll have to back off and wait. We can't call attention to ourselves. We need to wait until she's comfortable before we go any further."

"But shouldn't we contact the woman soon, just a nudge to keep her guessing." Becky wanted to get her hands on some money. She was tired of the living conditions and besides that she had a little 'habit' to support. She had hooked up with Danny because he had some grand idea of 'how to get our hands on some real money'.

"We don't want to rattle her nerves yet. Give her a little rope before we spring the trap."

"I don't see why you chose her. She's just a teacher. They don't make much money. We should try for some old rich broad who's about to kick the bucket. She wouldn't miss a few thousand. Besides she can't take it with her."

"That's precisely why I do the thinking. The rich broads you're talking about keep lawyers on their payroll just to make sure no one gets their hands on their money."

"Since you do all the thinking Mr. Hoity-Toity Dubois, what makes you so sure this teacher doesn't want to hang on to her money too? Why can't she hire a lawyer?"

"Because she won't have the money to hire a lawyer **and pay us,**" Danny was getting tired of her questions. He had thought of them himself but he didn't want Becky to know how unsure he was becoming of the whole scheme. They had spent a year working with his aunt's grandchild. He still owed the hypnotist. He couldn't back out now.

"I've done my homework. I have my ways. You'd be surprised what you can find out on the computer. I know how much she makes. She doesn't have a family to keep up. So she should have some socked away. Besides that, her rich aunt left her with some property she has yet to claim." Danny was explaining to Becky but he was also trying to bolster himself up as well. The plan had to work he had spent too much time and money to stop now. He couldn't let today's little glitch get in the way. He had to put Becky's concerns out of his head and concentrate on this small setback.

"You mean to tell me she'll be more willing to part with money she worked for and 'socked away' than the rich old lady who got it without lifting a finger?"

"You're giving me a headache with your stupid questions. Why don't you go to sleep?"

Becky was quiet for a while but she still couldn't get her thoughts to stop long enough to go to sleep, "So tell me just how much you think we can get out of 'What's her name' the teacher."

"**Becky**!" he yelled just as his cell phone made a brrrrr sound as it vibrated on the night stand.

"Subject left at one fifteen," Sally reported. It was very late when she saw Kayla leave with the child. She knew Danny was up to something but she didn't know what. He had paid her to watch and report. She was doing what she was paid to do but she was itching to find out what he was up to this time.

Danny had contacted Sally to do some surveillance work for him. "All I want you to do is watch at the mall entrance to see if this woman comes out with a child," were his instructions as he showed Kayla's picture. Using a long-range lens on his camera he had taken many pictures of Kayla. This one he had taken as she arrived at the school, her place of employment.

"Okay, so all I have to do is watch and report? That's all there is to it? Are you sure that's not against the law? I'm not going to jail for some stunt you pull."

"That's crazy. How can you get in trouble just looking to see who comes out of a place of business?"

"So what do I get out of this deal?"

"Well, I know you need a car because your car was totaled when you had that wreck. I could let you have my Volvo as payment. Becky and I have two. We can get along with one."

"You have two pieces of junk and you're willing to sacrifice one of them? My, aren't you generous."

"Take it or leave it."

"I don't have much choice. I do need a car right now such as it is. But I will be looking for another one. About anything will be better that that ugly old Volvo."

Sally had a habit of naming her cars so she decided to name this one 'Old Ugly'.

CHAPTER 4

SECURITY GUARDS
AND SANDY

Kayla looked down at the bundle as she slept, "Who are you little one? Do I look that much like your mother? She must be frantic by now. I tried to find her for you. You were no help by telling those people in the store that I was your mother. When I tried to tell them that I was not your mother, I was reprimanded severely, especially by one man. He threatened to call social services to report me. You're not mine but I would love to have a sweet child such as you."

Kayla reacted in shock at her own declaration, "I can't be thinking this way. If I happen to say that in front of the wrong people it could be taken the wrong way. They might think I want a child. I could be charged with taking this one. Oh my goodness! I could be charged with kidnapping!"

She shook her head as if to clear it and scolded herself, "I have to quit this line of thought and concentrate on what I can do to find your parents."

"What is it you are afraid of? Why did you react so when another person tried to comfort you? Why were you so afraid someone would take you away from me? Did something happen to your mother?"

The dream Kayla experienced had made her sit straight up in bed. In the dream she was being arrested for taking a child from the mall. Except for being arrested her dream was a reenactment of what actually happened the night before.

She was shopping for a dress to wear on her outing with Gabe. He had indicated he wanted to take her to a special place he had just heard about. They weren't really dating. They just went out together on Fridays.

It started out as something to do. They were both teachers at the same elementary school. One day they were in the teachers work room discussing their plans for the coming weekend. Since neither of them had plans they agreed to meet at a local restaurant that evening. After that the two of them had just evolved into a habit of getting together on Fridays.

Kayla had been meandering around in the boutique looking at the racks of dresses when a particular dress caught her eye. It was a formal dress that resembled one she had dreamed about in the past. Or was it a dream? It seemed so real. In the dream she was backstage with her aunt who was wearing a long flowing blue dress that had shiny stars that sparkled. Then she would wake up and there was no aunt. She was an orphan who lived in an orphanage. As a child she often pretended she was dressed in a pretty blue gown as she danced like her dream aunt.

"That color would look great on you and it would bring out the teal of your beautiful eyes."

Kayla jumped as the clerk walked up behind her. "I'm sorry I didn't hear you," she apologized for her reaction.

"Would you like to try it on?"

"*Why not?*" she thought. She had plenty of time. she wasn't to meet with Gabe until eight. She could go back to her childhood fantasy and try on the dress. It wasn't like she had anything else to do. She did her house cleaning on Saturday. She worked on her lesson plans on Sunday evening.

So she took the dress to the dressing room and slipped it on. It was pretty. She turned around and viewed herself in the three mirrors. It could even be a wedding dress. But she wasn't shopping for a wedding dress. There wasn't anyone in her circle of male friends that she would consider marriage material anyway. So she changed back into her street clothes and casually perused the other racks.

"I should be looking for a more appropriate dress for tonight," she told herself as she continued to search through the racks but there wasn't anything in particular that interested her. Nothing stood out and said, "I'm special. Choose me."

The child had just walked up from behind her, "Mommy," she said as took Kayla's hand, "I lost you when you went in to try on the dress."

Kayla stooped down and looked into bright blue eyes, "I'm not your mommy sweetheart but I'll help you find her. Why don't we find a salesperson to help us? Can you tell me your name?"

She looked up a Kayla with such a sweet smile as only a child of about two years of age can. "You're funny Mommy." She laughed, "Okay we'll play the game. What's your name?"

The response took Kayla by surprise. She didn't know what to think. She looked at the child and noticed her hair was a beautiful sandalwood color.

"Okay I'll just call you Sandy. How's that?" She took the child's hand and started toward the service counter.

Sandy took Kayla's hand with an act of total trust. She swung their clasped hands back and forth and walked on as if it was second nature for her. She seemed happy and full of life. That is until the security guard offered to take her to her office. She was terrified when Marge reached for her hand to lead her away.

Kayla with help from others at the mall had tried to find the child's mother but no one came to claim her. Marge, one of the malls security guards, spent several hours trying to find the parent. She went through surveillance tapes but found nothing. The child had just walked up to Kayla and took her hand. It was very late when they decided to call it a night. Since it was so late and the child had already reacted with fear when anyone tried to separate her from Kayla, she was allowed to go home with the woman she thought of as her Mommy. They all knew that there was a chance that this would further advance the notion that Kayla was her mother. But it seemed to be the best solution since the child was sleeping peacefully in Kayla's arms.

Social Service was not called because of the late hour and Kayla remembered how scared the child became when a man said Social Services should take the child.

Kayla choked back a tear as she recalled the incident --"No! No! Mommy, don't let them take me. I'll be good." She wrapped her arms around Kayla's legs and held on tight. "Please Mommy let's go home. I don't like what that mean man said."

*"Why did she say she would be good? Did someone take her mother away? What happened to her mother? Did she leave or maybe **die**?"*

The child did not even stir while Kayla undressed her for bed the night before. She had found one of her smallest T-shirts that could serve as a night shirt and slipped it over her head.

Kayla picked up the child's dress she had placed on the chair and inspected it for a name tag or label that would help find her family. Even though her clothes were of good quality there was nothing to indicate the company that made them.

Not only was there no way to trace the clothes, but Kayla thought it odd that the child had nothing with her. As one who was well aware of how children liked to have something to hold on to, Kayla was surprised that the child had nothing, no doll, no toy, no child's purse, nothing. Another thing out of the ordinary was her seemingly excessive fear of authority. Otherwise she appeared to be a pleasant, happy, healthy, and well cared for child.

She wanted the child to know where she was in case she woke up so Kayla left the door of the bathroom open while she showered. She put on a bathrobe and wrapped a towel around her wet hair. When she returned to the bedroom Sandy was stretching from her sleep.

"Morning Mommy," she said cheerfully, "You smell pretty."

"Thank you and good morning to you too," Kayla answered as she stretched out on the bed beside Sandy. Since her search the night before was fruitless, she thought she would try again to get at least some hint as to the identity of this child.

She took the little hands in hers and looked into her eyes, "Can you tell me your name?"

"Oh I always liked this game," she clapped her hands in glee, "My name's Sandy. What's your name?"

"Kayla," she answered thinking that would encourage the child to open up. Now do you have another name?"

"Do you have another name?"

"Well yes I do. I have two names. My two names are Kayla Adair. Now what are your two names?" she asked as she tickled Sandy in the ribs."

"Sandy Adair, Mommy you're silly," she giggled.

"What in the…," Kayla started but stopped when she saw the puzzled look on Sandy's face.

"This is getting me nowhere," she thought as she searched in the closet for something to wear. She pulled out a pair of beige pants and a powder blue blouse.

Sandy walked up beside her and looked up with loving eyes, "You smell like the black cherry soap you like so much. Can I use it so I can smell pretty too?"

She was shocked. How did this child know what kind of soap she used? She ordered her soap from a specialty shop. There was no way she should know that she used a special order of black cherry soap.

"This is getting weird and freaking me out. She was asleep when we got to my house last night. I didn't notice her getting up in the night and she was still sleeping when I woke up this morning. Am I going crazy or am I still dreaming?"

The doorbell rang just as she was about to admit she was crazy. Marge, the mall security guard, and another woman stood at the door.

"Miss Adair, this is Mrs. Goodman, my supervisor," Marge said as she introduced the woman, "May we come in?"

"Yes of course," she remembered Marge. "Come on in."

"Is the child still with you?"

"Yes, have you found out anything else about her?" Kayla answered hopefully. She was already fond of Sandy and wanted to find her parents before she become too attached.

"No but I just wanted to check on her to make sure she's Okay. May we speak with her?"

"Of course

"I hope you don't take this the wrong way but I ran your name through an identity check last night before you left with her."

"I totally understand. You don't know me or Sandy. It's only reasonable that you are concerned for her safety. That's as it should be. As a teacher of young children I know how important it is to keep them safe and secure."

"Sandy," Kayla called, "Would you come here please?"

The sound of tiny feet running could be heard, "Okay Mommy," she answered cheerfully.

As she rounded the doorway she jerked to a stop and stared in terror at the two uniformed women. She inched her way to Kayla and hid behind her as she held on to her legs.

"Why don't we sit down?" Kayla offered as she led Sandy over to the sofa and sat down beside her and held her hand. She motioned toward the chairs across from them for the others to sit there.

"It's okay," Kayla leaned over and patted Sandy on her legs, "Mrs. Goodman and Miss Brown just dropped in for a visit with us.

Sandy looked up at Kayla with trusting eyes, "Oh."

"Can you tell me your name?" Mrs. Goodman leaned toward Sandy and asked.

"Sandy," she answered softly as she squirmed and pushed further back against the sofa. She looked up at Kayla for encouragement.

"It's okay," Kayla drew her closer to her side.

"Do you have another name?"

Kayla winced when Sandy was asked this. The two of them had just had this conversation. It didn't look good for Kayla. *"I hope she doesn't answer 'Adair'. These women will think I've been rehearsing with her."*

Sandy looked up at Kayla with round questioning eyes, "Are they playing the game too?"

"I – uh, - this morning I was interrogating the child for the same reason as you are," Kayla hoped this explanation would suffice.

She also hoped Sandy didn't know what interrogating meant. She was intelligent that was for sure.

"Well what was the answer?" Mrs. Goodman asked Kayla.

"You ask her," Kayla threw it back at her, "She wants to know if you are playing a game with her."

"Okay let's play the game. Sandy is your first name. What is your other name?"

"What is **your** other name?" Sandy seemed to gather strength from Kayla and was now playing hard ball.

Mrs. Goodman sat up straight in her chair. Patience wasn't her best trait. That's why she left a lot of the foot work to those under her supervision.

"Sandy shows a lot of spunk for one that seems to be afraid of a badge," Kayla thought as she hid her grin behind her hand.

"My name is Mrs. Goodman," she said in exasperation, "Now Sandy what is your other name?"

Kayla was waiting for Sandy's answer to be 'Mrs. Goodman'. She remembered when she questioned Sandy about her other name Sandy had asked Kayla what her other name was and Kayla told her it was Adair. So when Kayla asked again what her other name was her answer had been the same last name as Kayla's, Adair.

Kayla smiled sheepishly as she expected Sandy to say 'Mrs. Goodman' in a patronizing voice. But to her surprise her answer was a sweet positive, "Adair".

"Where do you live?"

"Here with Mommy," was the sharp reply.

She looked up at Kayla and announced, "I don't want to play this game anymore." Then she slid off the couch and toddled back to the bedroom.

It was apparent the conversation -which was more like an inquisition-was over.

"I'm sorry," Kayla apologized, "I don't know what to say. I haven't been able to get anything out of her either. She keeps insisting that I'm her mother and this is her home."

"Well I guess we've been dismissed, "Marge laughed, "The situation is odd. She seems to be happy and fits right here with you as if she is home. She certainly treats you like you are her mother."

"I hope you understand that we have to report this to the authorities. Otherwise we could be held liable," Mrs. Goodman announced as she got up to leave. There didn't appear to be any reason to stay.

"Dear Lord," Kayla prayed, "What am I going to do? I'm in desperate need of Your help. I don't mean to be pushy but I need help **now.**"

Chapter 5

KAYLA'S FRIEND TALITHA

After Marge and Mrs. Goodman, the mall security guards, left Kayla was unsure as to what to do with Sandy. She had not told them about the other revelations that came from Sandy. She was not about to let them know that Sandy knew a lot more about Kayla than any of them knew about Sandy.

Sandy had settled down as if she belonged there in Kayla's house. She seemed content to be there even though there was nothing in the house that belonged to her -No toys, no huggy-blanket, nothing. She didn't even have a change of clothes.

"What am I going to do? This child needs something else to wear. She's not my child but I just can't let her keep wearing the same clothes she has on."

Kayla walked through every room in the house pacing the floor trying to figure out what to do. When she went back into the bedroom she found Sandy sitting on the floor turning the pages of a book she must have taken from Kayla's bookshelf. During the summer Kayla shopped for new children's books for her second grade class. She always reviewed the books before she used them at school. That's the reason she had so many children's books there on her bookshelf.

Since Sandy seemed to be settled and content to peruse the books, Kayla called her best friend, "Talitha I need help," she gasped.

"What in the world is wrong? You sound terrible. Has anything happened? You were alright yesterday when you said you were going shopping."

"Was that yesterday? So much has happened since then. It seems like a year has passed."

"Did you have a fight with Gabe? Never mind I'm coming right over."

"Prepare to be shocked," Kayla said to the dead phone.

"Gabe! Oh dear! Sandy's appearance put a big hole in everything. I was in the midst of shopping for a fancy dress to wear to that fancy new restaurant he has been raving about. We were going there last night. I totally forgot about our date when Sandy appeared out of nowhere. Her entrance into my life changed everything. It was like she just was continuing on a normal day of her life with me. She even asked why I didn't buy the formal dress she liked."

She picked up the phone to call Gabe when she noticed the light blinking on her answering machine. It was Gabe. He had left a terse message about being stood up. Her return call went to his answering machine. She left a short message of apology and a promise to explain later.

Fifteen minutes later there was a loud banging at Kayla's door. Talitha didn't wait for Kayla to open the door fully. She pushed her way in the door Kayla was opening.

"What's wrong?" she wheezed. She was out of breath from rushing over.

"Come with me," Kayla turned and headed for the bedroom. There sat Sandy still content as she continued to look at the books scattered around her.

"What the-…? When did you get a child?"

"Yesterday when I went shopping."

"Since when did they start selling children at the boutique?"

"It's a long story. I'll tell you after you help me find this child some clothes."

"You mean clothes didn't come with it."

"As I said it's a long story and even though it's odd it really isn't funny. I need help not sarcasm."

"Mommy, who is this woman? Why is she laughing? Did you say something funny?"

"Mommy?" Talitha stopped looking down at the child and swung her head around. Her attention was now focused on Kayla.

"It's a long story."

"You've already said that, several times by the way."

"Sandy, this is Talitha, my best friend. Do you have a best friend?"

"Yes, you are my best friend, Mommy."

"Well it was worth a shot," muttered Kayla.

"What was that all about?" Talitha was thoroughly confused. "I know. I know. It's a long story. And you'll tell me after we go shopping. So let's get this shopping over with so I can hear this long story."

"Oh dear," Kayla remarked as they started to leave. She looked up at dark clouds hanging in the sky. "I'd better go back in and get a rain coat."

"And I'll get my umbrella out of my car," Talitha added as she headed for her car.

The rain was really pouring down when they got to the department store so Kayla put Sandy under her coat as they ran to the front door. Kayla took off the dripping wet rain coat as Talitha put her umbrella in a plastic that was provided at the entrance. They skirted around the 'caution wet floor' sign and headed for the children's clothing department.

The shopping trip was a disaster. Shopping for a child was foreign to Kayla so she didn't know where to start. The clerks who were trying to be helpful kept asking questions and Kayla had no clue what the answers were. So Sandy answered most of them which brought inquisitive looks her way. Kayla didn't know how long Sandy would be with her so she bought only one complete outfit and night clothes. Then she thought of the child not having anything of her own to play with. She asked Sandy if she wanted a toy or maybe a doll.

"Yes please," she answered politely. She went over and picked out a doll that resembled her. It had sandy hair and blue eyes like she did.

"Kayla most children eat a snack about this time. Don't you think we need to get something for Sandy?" Talitha asked. She knew Kayla was aware of this fact but apparently with all that had happened to her she had just forgotten. And she was still waiting for the 'long story'.

Kayla decided that a public place like a restaurant was not the place to tell her story. She thought a park would be much better. Sandy could play while they set up a picnic lunch. So they went grocery shopping to let Sandy pick out what she wanted to eat.

"I have no idea what you like to eat." She said to Sandy as they stood in line at the deli.

A woman standing in line behind them smiled when Kayla told Sandy to pick out what she wanted.

The woman's smile turned to a frown when Sandy said "Okay Mommy."

She had just heard Kayla say that she had no idea what she liked to eat. She didn't mean to say anything but the words just came out, "You don't know what your own child likes to eat?"

"She's not my - … excuse me," Kayla took the order and left with Sandy and Talitha before the woman said anything else. She didn't give Talitha a chance to confront the woman which could have made things worse.

As they left the deli Kayla heard part of the judgmental conversation between the others who were still in line.

"What kind of mother doesn't know what her child likes to eat?"

'She must not see her very often."

"Maybe she doesn't have custody and sees her once in a while. That must be the child's chaperone with her."

By that time, they were in no mood to go to a park so they decided to eat at home.

"Since we're going home instead of the park, I need to shop for 'child food'. I don't have anything at home for a child. What do children eat anyway?" she asked Talitha.

"Why don't we let her pick it out? If it turns out to be all sweets, we can nix it.

There were no confrontations at the grocery. Most of the shoppers were used to children reaching for their favorites.

After lunch Kayla put Sandy on her bed for a nap. "Sleep tight sweetheart," she whispered as she tucked the sheet under her chin and placed the doll next to her.

"That's one thing I do know. Children take naps after lunch."

After hearing the story Talitha laughed, "Looks like you're a kid napper."

"Talitha your play on words really isn't funny. I could be in a lot of trouble. I couldn't find the parent and she kept insisting I was her mother. A man even called me a name and threatened to call social service to take her away because I kept saying I wasn't her mother. It was like the people at the deli. They look at me like I'm a terrible mother. **And I'm not even a mother.**"

"You have to calm down, Kayla. Your nerves are shot," Talitha consoled her.

"I haven't even told you the weirdest thing yet. Talitha, she knew the name of soap I use even before she even saw it. How did she know that?"

"That's it. You must look like her mother and you use the same soap she does. So you smell and look like her. That's why she thinks you are her mother.

"You're grasping at straws and you know it. A child knows her own mother."

"Yes and she says **you** are her mother."

"Okay back to the soap. Her mother can't use the same soap. I order soap from a specialty shop which makes mine exclusively for me. That's why it shocked me when she knew it was black cherry."

"Only the Lord knows what else she knows about me. The whole situation is crazy? It's not only crazy it's spooky. If I'm still dreaming I wish I would wake up soon before they carry me off in a white jacket with arms tied in the back."

"You're not crazy and this is no dream. Maybe she just recognized the smell."

"That would make sense if she smelled cherry but **black** cherry? I don't think so."

"Okay you're right that is stretching it a bit."

"Tell me, what should I do? Do you think I should go back to the boutique?"

"Have you called to see if there is an amber alert for a missing child?"

"That's just it. The child isn't missing, she's found. How would it look if I call the police and reported a found child and she 'followed me home'? Besides the security guards came here early this morning to check on Sandy. They didn't say anyone was looking for her."

"We'll just have to sit down and reason this out. *But I have no earthly idea how to do that.*"

Talitha convinced Kayla to let her spend the night with her. They sat up all night trying to get their minds off the situation. They tried to watch a movie. They got out old photo albums. They baked cookies. But it was no use the 'situation' was asleep in Kayla's bed.

"She took the child shopping and bought her some clothes. Then went to the grocery store," Sally reported to Danny. "By the way Old Ugly you palmed off on me nearly croaked on me while I was following them. It needs a tune up and the tires are as slick as your bald head. I need some of the money you promised me **now**."

"Okay, okay don't blow a gasket, calm down. Come by. I can let you have enough to get Old Ugly, as you call the car, serviced. I have another little errand for you to run anyway."

"It seems to be working even though that stunt you pulled at the mall almost threw a wrench in our plans." Danny couldn't help poking the jibe at Becky. "Now go to the mall and type the note just as I told you. I need it here when Sally comes. No wait. I'll go type the note myself. This is too important to take a chance. You stay here and wait for Sally."

CHAPTER 6

LUTHER MEETS JOE

Luther was sitting at the bar mulling over his situation. He was short on cash. His last job had not netted him half as much as he had been promised by his fence. That's when Joe came in and slammed his fist on the counter and ordered a beer. The bartender had put up with about all he could take that day. So he told him to take his beer and attitude over to a table in a far corner.

Luther didn't believe in coincidences but he did believe in luck. When the opportunity arose it was up to him to take advantage of it. This seemed to be one of the times to seize the moment. This guy was certainly open for someone to talk to, someone who was willing to let him vent. He had met some of his best cohorts in a bar.

After waiting for him to settle in and begin to fume Luther decided Joe was ready to explode and would be ready to tell his trouble to almost anyone who would listen. Luther picked up his beer and ambled over, "Looks like you could use some company, my friend."

Joe leaned his chair back and scowled at him, but slid his foot under the table and shoved out the chair opposite him, "Suit yourself."

They sat in silence for a while. Luther was a patient man and knew when to let an angry man be. He prided himself in the fact he could read a person's moods and knew just how far he could push. He was right. It took a few minutes.

Joe was too angry to hold it in any longer. He had been stewing all day since 'Mr. big-shot O'Malley' had fired him. "What does he mean 'I wasn't pulling my weight? I worked my butt off for that old man. I don't need his old job anyway I just took it because Mom insisted."

O'Malley Construction Company was large, one of the largest in the country. The buildings itself covered thirty-eight acres. They had several security guards but they were mainly there to protect the company against law suits in case someone, especially a child, slipped onto the grounds through the wire fence and got hurt. That's why they patrolled the perimeter of the fence. There was only one guard at the front gate and one at the main office.

The owner of the company Arthur O'Malley was a good man who paid his workers a fair wage. But he expected his workers to earn the wages and his respect. He in turn respected his employees. They were like family. Arthur was of the old school. He didn't trust banks. So he paid his workers in cash a well-kept secret. That is until Luther met Joe Bigalow one of the few men who was ever fired.

Joe was hired when his mother, a faithful employee for years, had been diagnosed with cancer. Arthur thought if he hired Joe he would help his mother. But Joe failed to live up to his mother's standards. His work record was so bad Arthur had no choice but to let him go.

They sat and talked until the wee hours of the night. Luther did very little talking he mainly listened. He listened and learned. What he learned may help in his next caper. Luther filed away in his mind the information Joe had shared.

"I need to do some thinking," Luther told himself as he walked to his car which was a 'loaner'. He didn't really have transportation except for loaners. He liked to be unencumbered in case he had to move away quickly. That's why he would not finance anything. So when he needed one he would borrow a car from an associate who ran a used cars business otherwise known as chop shops.

He waited a few days and decided to visit the bar again on a chance that Joe might be there trying to drown his woes in a bottle of beer.

Luck was on his side. Joe was there in the back corner where he was the first time Luther met him. Two empty bottles were in front of him to testify how long he had been sitting there. Luther ordered a beer and went over and sat down without an invitation. Joe groused about life in general for a while then he began talking about his financial problems.

"The old man who owns my apartment has been hounding me for rent. How am I supposed to pay him when I don't have money? Heck I don't even have money to buy food much less pay rent. Then I get this notice from the finance company. If I don't come up with two month's payments they're going to repossess my car. I've been keeping it hidden so they won't be able to get their hands on it. But I don't know how long that'll work. I guess I could try to sell it before they find me or it."

Luther was an opportunist. He remembered Joe bragging about his new car the last time they talked. If he helped Joe now maybe it would pay off later.

"Well now maybe I can help you there. Where do you have it stashed?"

Joe's countenance changed immediately. This could mean things were looking up. He jumped up from the chair ready to sell.

"You want to buy my Charger?"

Then he sat back down. He loved that car. It made him feel like he was somebody when he was behind the wheel of his Phantom Black Pearl Dodge Charger. "I don't want to sell it. But what choice do I have?"

"I don't need a car right now but I know some people," getting Al to **buy** a car would be a first for Luther.

"I can't help you with your housing problem. But I've had some dealings with cars," he grinned at his own joke because he had stolen a few. He stood up to go before Joe had another change of heart. "Now where is this car of yours?"

"I parked it out back, pulled it between the fence and two rusted out junkers that have been there for a few years. The repo guys wouldn't think to look there."

He knew the value had decreased when he walked out of the dealership. But after paying off the loan he hoped he could get enough left to pay his rent.

"Nice car. I tell you what, let me contact a pal who deals with used cars and see what he can give you for the car. Why don't you leave it here and I'll get back to you in a couple of hours?"

Luther needed to do some thinking. There had to be some way he could use this opportunity to his advantage. He contacted Al to see if he was interested. Luther had never met Al in person. He contacted him by the cell phone that Al supplied. It was set up so he could only call Al or one of Al's employees. Luther was a free-lance person. He found his own 'jobs' and contacted Al when he had something he thought Al would be interested in. So he called Al.

"Carry it by the fix-it shop and I'll have Bo take a look at it." He was told. Bo managed Bert's Fix-it Shop which also served as a front for Al's chop shop.

Al was used to dealing with stolen vehicles and payed his 'help' just enough to keep them working for him.

"Al said he can't pay you that much money for a car even if it's legit." Bo told him.

So Luther put the word out on the street that he had a car to sell.

"This is the real kicker, this one isn't hot," he laughed when he told his contact.

When his idea of getting Al to buy the car fell through Luther went back to tell Joe.

"That's my luck. Now what am I going to do? My own mother kicked me out of our house. If I don't pay rent on that fleabag I am staying at today, I won't have a place to stay. Now they're going to take my car. It's O'Malley's fault for firing me. Today's payday I can see the old biddies now counting out the measly salary he pays. Good riddance I say. Who needs his old job?"

"Oh boy he must have tied one on after I left probably celebrating my selling his car for him. Now he'll be trying to drown his sorrows because Al didn't want it. What does he expect? I can't find a buyer on such short notice. I just thought Al would be interested. How on earth do I find such losers?"

Luther was about to walk out when he remembered Joe saying something about 'O'Malley paying his workers in cash'. He sat back down and listened to Joe go on and on about his bad luck. Every once in a while he would ask a question that might lead to more information. He didn't know just what he would do with the info but he listened and filed it away in his brain. He would sort it out later.

"Why don't you go home and we'll talk again tomorrow. In the meantime I'll drive your Charger around and let some of my contacts know it's for sale but it may take a little longer to find a buyer.

A few days later Al contacted Luther. He decided he could use Joe's car after all. He needed one or two straight sales to make his business transactions appear legal.

"Go by Al's Junk Yard and get the money for the car. Don't bring Joe with you," were his instructions. "The less he knows the better it would be for everyone. Get him to sign the title but don't fill out the transfer. Then carry the car to Fred's Car Lot. Don't worry about the paperwork they'll fill it out."

Luther followed the directions to Al's Junk Yard which was on the far west side of town outside the city limits. He entered the yard and couldn't help but notice ruts made by the wide warped and rusted wrought-iron gate that was leaning to one side. He looked around in search of a building or an office. All he could see were pile after pile of rusting junk metal. A pathway of sorts was hard packed dirt between the piles. He could hear the crusher working so he worked his way around the maze of metal as he headed toward the noise. He jumped just in time to escape being hit with a front-end loader filled with scrap metal. "Hey," yelled the driver of the dozer, "Watch where you're going!"

"I'm looking for Al," Luther quickly recovered his composure and yelled to be heard over the roar of the vehicle.

"Al? Did you say Al?"

"Yes Al. I came to see Al."

The man seemed puzzled but reached for his two-way radio. "There's someone here to see an Al."

After a minute of silence, he shrugged his shoulders and told Luther, "Someone will be out shortly."

Luther was startled when a man materialized in front of him. He melded with the piles. His coveralls, face, and even his hair were the same color as the mountains of rusting scrap.

"Are you Al?" Luther had never met his contact, Al, and was hoping this would be his chance to see the man behind the voice on the phone.

The man didn't answer the question. He just fixed his rusty eyes on Luther.

"Here this is what you came for," the raspy voice blended in with the site. Even his voice was rusty. He reached out a fist of gnarled fingers and handed Luther an envelope, turned around, and left in the same direction he came. He disappeared - just faded away back into the piles of scrap.

Luther was glad to be leaving. Normally he wasn't skittish. But this wasn't a place he wanted to be. It felt good to be out in the open spaces. He could breathe better. He could even think clearer.

"Well that's odd. What little he did say didn't sound at all like the Al I talk with on the phone. Oh well, I didn't go there for conversation. I went to get money for Joe's car. I suppose that's what's in the envelope."

Joe was not happy when he opened the envelope. "This is barely enough to cover the payoff on the car and pay half of my rent. Now what am I going to do?"

"Look you can't be choosey. You were about to lose the car anyway."

Luther still had the keys and started out the door to deliver the car to Fred's Car Lot. As he was leaving, he made a spur of the moment decision. He took a page from Al's book- the fewer people who knew him the better it would be. He would get someone else to deliver the car. Then he would meet with Joe again. He had already invested a lot of time with him. So what harm would a little more time cause?

"I have to deliver the car now but we can figure out something when I get back."

Luther called his friend Jose' to see if he would do him a favor.

"Is it legit? You know I don't deal with stolen goods."

"The only thing I want you to do is go with me to deliver a car to Fred's Auto. I just need a ride back home. And no, the car is not stolen. I have the title right here."

Jose' was happy to take Luther up on the offer to let him drive the Charger.

So Luther drove Jose's car to Fred's Car Lot. Jose' followed him in the Charger.

It took them an hour to find the lot which was located on eastern side near the edge of the city. When they finally arrived at the car lot Fred, who busy with a customer, asked Sally to help him until he was free. Luther left Jose' with the Charger and title and wandered around looking as if he was interested in a vehicle.

Sally ushered Jose' into the office because Luther was nowhere to be found. She took the title and finished filling out the transfer to Fred's Used Cars.

"Thanks Joe," she said, "Now let's take a look at your, I mean our car."

"I'm not ... ." Jose' started. "*Oh well what difference does it make?*"

"She thought I was Joe," Jose' laughed as they drove away, "I thought she would never stop talking and finish the transaction. She was telling me how she would love to have the Charger. How her old Volvo keeps breaking down and the mechanic tells her it's a pile of junk not worth hauling in."

Joe was still at the bar when Luther returned. He didn't really know why but he had decided to Loan Joe money to help pay the rent.

"I tell you what I'll loan you the money to pay the rest of the rent. You can pay me back when you get a job. You are looking for a job aren't you?"

Luther wasn't being charitable he just wanted to have an excuse to continue talking with Joe. He didn't know what would be important but he felt the more information he got the better off he would be. Luther, the opportunist, had his ears open to anything that may come his way. He gathered information and filed it away in his brain. There were times when it came in handy.

Sally took one look at the Charger. It was love at first sight. She just had to have that car. She was sick of Old Ugly. That's what she called the Volvo she got from Danny. It took some fast talking but she finally persuaded Fred to sell her the car.

She couldn't afford the Charger but she made a financial agreement with Fred. She would pay on time until she got enough for a down payment. She really wanted the car. Until then she still had Old Ugly.

"This old pile of junk has had it," the mechanic told Sally, "I'll try to get it running but it won't last long." The Volvo had stopped running right in the middle of the road as she was on her way home.

Fred let her drive one of his older cars while the Volvo was in the shop, "You have just one more payment to have enough for a down payment on the Charger. After that I'll transfer the title to you. But I'll still have a lien, of course."

"And it will be headed to Bert's Fix-it Shop to be painted Cobalt Blue," Sally promised herself, "I love everything about the car except the color. Pearl Black looks like a gangster's car."

CHAPTER 7

EXTORTION LETTER

Kayla and Talitha bumped heads as they were jerked awake by the ringing phone. They had fallen asleep leaning against each other just before the sun came up. Photo albums were scattered over the coffee table. The smell of cookies lingered in the air. They had tried to think of a way to solve the problem. When that didn't work they tried to find a way to forget the problem. They had listened to music. They cooked cookies. The movie they tried to watch didn't help. Looking at old photo albums worked for a little while. Then their minds went back to the child who was fast asleep in Kayla's bed. They needed to get some sleep. That didn't happen until just before dawn.

Kayla stumbled from the couch in search for her phone which was still ringing.

"Hello," she answered in a sleep induced husky voice then she cleared her throat and answered again, "Hello," She squeaked.

"Kayla, is that you? Are you alright?" Reverend Vernon Miller asked. *"If I didn't know her better I'd swear she was suffering from a hang-over."*

"I uh I'm fine," she croaked, "Ahem," and cleared her throat again.

"Are you sure? You don't sound fine?"

"Yes I'm fine," Kayla tried to speak in a normal voice even though she still sounded like she had just awakened, which she had.

"I called because I was worried about you. When you didn't show up at church this morning I thought something must have happened. You always come early for church especially when you're in charge of setting up Communion. This is not like you."

"Oh!" Kayla reacted in disbelief, "What day is it? Is it Sunday already? I'm so sorry."

"Don't worry about it we have it covered. I'm just worried about you."

"I – uh something suddenly came up that caused me to lose track of time."

She paused to collect her thoughts. It had been a rough night and she was still suffering from the lack of sleep.

"It must have been something drastic to cause her to forget what day it is," he thought to himself, *"She must not want to talk about it. Otherwise she would explain without me asking."*

"I need time to sort out a few things. Please bear with me for a while until I get back into the swing of things."

"Does that mean you won't even be attending church services? *It sure sounds like it.* What can I do to help?" The preacher asked with concern.

Kayla thought for a moment. Then it dawned on her. She couldn't possibly attend church. She had Sandy. She would be calling her 'Mommy' if she carried her with her. How would she explain **that** to the church members?

"Boy! That would give them something to talk about for months," she laughed.

Then she snapped back to the question the preacher had asked.

"It would be a great help if I am relieved of my duties while I attend to the matter."

"What?...Uh... *This must be more serious that I thought.* Are you sure I can't do something to help?"

"No, no I'll be fine. I just need some time."

"Of course now don't you worry about a thing, we'll handle things on this end. But you must promise to let us know if there's anything we can do to help. Remember I have wide shoulders if you want to talk."

"I need a strong cup of coffee," Kayla looked over at Talitha, "How about you?"

"I'm in and I guess we need to fix breakfast for the little mystery child," Talitha began searching in the cabinets to see what they could fix for breakfast while Kayla was busy with making coffee. "We could always eat cookies. We have plenty of **them**."

While Talitha was deciding what to fix, Kayla went into the bedroom to check on Sandy. She was sitting on the floor singing to her doll.

"Did you like that song, Sandy?" she asked the doll. "When I grow up I'm going to sing in the choir just like Mommy."

Kayla backed out of the room and rushed back to the kitchen.

"She knows I sing in the choir, Talitha."

"That does it. Now we get down to business. This child will plead for mercy when I get through with my interrogation." Talitha stopped her search for breakfast fixings and turned a no-nonsense look on Kayla.

"I don't think that will work. She has a way of turning every question I ask back to me. By the end of the day you'll be the one pleading for mercy."

"Back to plan B, whatever that is. Let's concentrate on that coffee and breakfast. I'll make a western omelet with eggs, bacon, cheese, peppers, and anything else I can find in the refrigerator. I need brain food!"

They spent the rest of the day letting Sandy take the lead. They steered away from asking direct questions but led the conversation toward things they thought would give some insight as to her background – background that a child could have made in two or three years.

They did learn a few things. For one so young the child had a large vocabulary, was articulate in her speech, and had a good command of the language. It was obvious she had been living with someone who was well educated and spent a lot of time communicating with her. But they were no closer to finding out her identity.

The preacher's curiosity was getting the best of him. He felt he knew his flock well especially Kayla. She was not a secretive person.

"Kayla was so allusive when I talked with her," he told his wife, Elaine. "She said she needed time to attend to personal business. Do you think she has a medical problem that she would rather not discuss with a man? Maybe she needs to talk with a woman. Do you think you could go over there and find out?"

She didn't want to meddle in Kayla's business but she went to appease her husband.

"Vernon that was embarrassing. When I knocked on her door Kayla answered it but she stood in the doorway and did not invite me in. She apologized and told me it was not a good time for a visit. She must have indicated to you that she didn't want to talk about it. She has a right to her privacy. I hope you never ask me to do anything like that ever again!"

She didn't tell him that Kayla shut the door in her face when a child ran up behind her and called her Mommy. She planned to apologize to her about the intrusion but she didn't know how to go about it without appearing nosy.

Monday morning Kayla was groggy from the lack of sleep. She had not slept well in two days. On top of that her phone rang throughout the night. It would ring just once so the indicator showed no ID. Her nerves were in a knot. Her mind kept going back to all the things that had happened in just three days. Everything started on Friday evening when she went shopping. It started out as a pleasant event. Then it turned into a mystery. Who was this sweet child who called her Mommy? As the days progressed it turned into a hunt. They hunted for a parent. Then things turned nasty. At the mall a man verbally attacked her about her role as a mother. People she did not know were making false judgements about her.

Saturday morning Sandy's revelations were a shock. She knew too much about Kayla. Sandy's answers to Kayla's questions did not shed any light on the subject. Then the security guards came by to check on Sandy. They had not found any clues as to Sandy's family. Then later that day when she and Tabitha carried Sandy shopping for clothes and groceries customers in the stores made snide remarks about her as a parent.

She had been so befuddled she had not realized it was Sunday until Rev. Miller called about her commitment to set up communion. After talking to him she knew the preacher was concerned but what could she say that would not take a long time to try to explain. She knew the preacher had sent his wife to check on her when Elaine knocked on her door. She was still feeling guilty about not inviting Elaine in when she came by Sunday afternoon to check on her.

All this was weighing heavily on her mind as she sorted her morning mail. She thought nothing of the letter with no return address. But when she opened it a picture fell out. She bent down to pick it up and saw it was a picture of her walking out of the mall with Sandy asleep in her arms. The message that came with the picture read, *"I saw you kidnap the child which by the way is a federal offence. $500,000 in used bills will keep me quiet and **you out of federal prison**. You have one week. I'll send details later."*

"Half a million dollars! Somebody wants me to give them half a million dollars! This is ridiculous! Why would anyone think I'd just hand them half a million dollars? I'm not that crazy. I don't have that kind of money anyway!"

"Mommy, why are you yelling?" Sandy came running into the room.

"It's nothing," Kayla quickly tried to hide her angry frustration as she led her toward the kitchen, "Why don't we have pancakes for breakfast?"

Kayla tried to calm her nerves as her first bite of syrup-covered pancake headed toward her mouth. She jumped at the sound of the doorbell ringing which made her drop the pancaked fork. The syrupy pancake dribbled down her pajamas and landed on the floor. She ran to the sink, wet her hands, and grabbed at a paper towel and yanked. The sheet didn't tear off instead a long trail of towels followed her to the door.

Two women stood at the door. Before they could say anything Kayla snapped, "Whatever you're selling I'm not interested! It's too early to be disturbed **and** as you can see I'm not even dressed yet."

Kayla slammed the door just as the telephone rang.

"What now?" She stormed as she reached to answer and swept a strand of hair away from her face. In doing so her hair got stuck on her syrupy hand.

"Damn," Kayla muttered as she held the phone to her ear.

"Mommy!" the surprised Sandy reprimanded.

"Miss Adair?" the shocked voice sounded over the phone.

The doorbell rang again.

Kayla yelled as she threw up her fists full of paper towels. This made Sandy scream and cry at the same time.

A voice on the unattended phone said, "Hang on I'm calling 911."

"I heard screams coming from the house," Marge told the dispatcher. She had called to check on Kayla and Sandy.

"Honey, it's okay," Kayla sank down to the floor and took her in her arms to comfort her. She felt so badly about scaring Sandy she started to cry as well.

The two women at the door heard the scream and rushed in. They found Kayla on the floor rocking back and forth with Sandy in her arms. Sandy was still screaming. Kayla was in a disheveled mess. Her hair was tangled and matted to her head, her pajamas were sticky with syrup and her eyes were red from crying.

"What are you doing to this child?" one of the women shouted as they wrestled Sandy away from Kayla's arms.

A few minutes later police with blue lights flashing and siren blaring screeched to a halt at the house. Following close behind were EMS, Marge from mall security, and a news hound. Neighbors rushed out to see what was happening. Talitha pulled in just as Kayla was being wheeled out.

The news hound Nathanael Harbinger had heard the 911 call on his scanner and raced to the address. It's something police officers don't appreciate especially when a reporter shows up before they even have a chance to see if there is an emergency.

It was Nathanael's habit to follow any lead no matter how mundane it may seem at the time. Some of his best scoops came from this habit. Sometimes a good story started out as a no brainer, an ordinary daily routine event. He was nicknamed Nat-the-Hound because he dogged a story until it either panned out or came to nothing.

The next day there on the front page was a picture of a disheveled, disoriented, sticky pajama-clad, Kayla being taken from her house by EMS. The story that followed had little substance just a lot of supposition. It was about a little girl in the arms of someone from social services crying for her mother as the mother was wheeled out by EMS.

"The week's not up yet," were the first words out of her mouth when Kayla came out of the medically induced sleep. "The letter said I had a week."

CHAPTER 8

KAYLA 'KIDNAPPER' IN NEWS

"What did you mean the week is not up yet?" Talitha asked Kayla as she helped her get dressed to go home from the hospital. "Something else must have happened. How much could have happened in the few hours I was gone? Don't answer that. A lot must have. You're in the hospital. The morning paper has your picture plastered over the front page."

She had brought Kayla a change of clothes because she had been transported by EMS in her pajamas which were a sticky mess.

"Talitha you don't know the half of it. If you thought it was weird before, wait until you hear the last. At least I hope it is the last."

Then she remembered the pandemonium of the day before. "Do you know where Sandy is? What happened to her? I'm afraid I scared her to death when I went mad from all the craziness that happened."

"She's in the hands of social services. She went ballistic when they took her away. I was just coming back to your house when I ran into the frenzied spectacle at your house. What happened?"

"I don't know. It happened so fast. I was bombarded. A woman yelled at me and Sandy was snatched out of my arms. A policeman came up and talked with the woman who had Sandy. Before I knew what was happening I was placed on a stretcher by paramedics. I tried frantically to fight them off but I was strapped down and hauled away. Everything and everybody seemed to be coming at me from all sides. Listen to me. I sound like a paranoid schizophrenic. It's a wonder they let me leave the hospital."

It had taken a lot of persuasion on Talitha's part for the hospital to release Kayla. She told them if Kayla was crazy then she was too. But she would tell her that later after she got her settled back home. "It's a wonder they didn't keep us both on the psycho ward."

It had been such a crazy few days they were quiet on the drive home.

"What's this?" Talitha asked as she picked up the picture from the floor where it had fallen again."

"That's the first thing that happened yesterday. It's a pay up or else note."

"A what?"

"Read it for yourself.

Tabitha read, "*I saw you kidnap the child which by the way is a federal offence. $500,000 in used bills will keep me quiet and you out of federal prison. You have one week. I'll send details later.*"

"It seems to be a ransom note where you pay to keep the victim instead of the other way around." Kayla threw out her hands in disbelief, "After all that has happened since then, that note doesn't scare me anymore. It makes me mad!"

"Why don't you sit down while I fix us a pot of coffee?" Talitha pulled a chair out from the kitchen table and indicated for Kayla to sit.

"Talk to me," she said as she turned and walked toward the sink.

"My nerves were already shot from reading the letter. I scared Sandy when I yelled 'half a million dollars'. So I put the letter aside and tried to calm down by fixing pancakes for breakfast. We had just started to eat when the doorbell rang causing me to spill syrup all over myself. I yelled at two women at the door for soliciting that early in the morning. Just as I was closing the door the phone rang. As I answered it syrup from my hand got in my hair. Then the doorbell rang again. When I screamed in frustration Sandy started to scream as well. I don't know who called the paramedics. It all turned into a circus and I was the clown. And who in the world let in that idiot from the newspaper?"

"It was a mad house when I arrived on the scene," Talitha explained. "I didn't follow you to the hospital because of the raucous. I thought I needed to stay there to see what was going on. Well that was a mistake. I still don't know what happened. Sandy was 'holding her own' as she fought a woman who was trying to subdue her. I didn't like it one bit so I tried to rescue Sandy. The woman informed me she was from social services and unless I had legal claim she was taking Sandy into protective custody.

"I still wasn't convinced. I told her I needed to see some form of ID. 'Lucille, show this woman our credentials, I have my hands full,' she said. She must have been one of the women who rang your doorbell. She said something about a door being slammed in her face and you trying to harm the child. Then a woman who identified herself as Marge came up to me. She had heard the exchange. When I told her I was your best friend, she told me she's the one who called 911. She called to warn you that her superior had reported the mall incident to the authorities. A lawyer had warned her about being liable. Then she heard you and Sandy scream. Evidently you dropped the phone but she could still hear screaming. So she called 911 and rushed over to see about you."

"Well even though that explains some of it I don't feel much better. I hope Sandy is okay. The poor child must be scared out of her wits."

"Social services" was the answer when Kayla called to check on Sandy, "May I help you?"

"Yes I'm calling about a child that was taken into custody yesterday."

"What is your name please?"

"I'm Kayla Adair."

"What is the name of the child you are inquiring about? And what is your relationship?"

"Oh dear, now how do I answer that? I should have thought this out before I called." Kayla reprimanded herself.

"She calls herself Sandy Adair. I just want to know if she's all right."

"Let me transfer you to another department. Hold on please."

After about five minutes a woman answered, "Miss Adair I can't give you any information and I suggest you to refrain from calling here again. It would be in your best interest."

"I just want to know how the child is."

"Good-day Miss Adair!" The phone went dead.

"I feel like I need to do something. But what can I do? She isn't my child."

Talitha looked around the room, "The place feels empty, doesn't it? She was here only a few days but she filled it up."

"I didn't ask for any of this. I was doing just fine going along minding my own business. Then 'boom' I was bowled over with this, whatever this is. All of a sudden my life has been turned upside down. A ray of sunshine came into my life and broke into the mundane existence I was living. I didn't even realize how boring my life had become until she came. Maybe God sent her to dig me out of the rut I had made for myself."

"Don't beat yourself up. You are a respected member of society, a good teacher, a hard worker in the church. You're always ready to help the less fortunate in the community. You are a good person, Kayla."

"Well then, why do I feel so rotten?"

The next morning's news made her feel worse. The headlines read "Teacher Accused of Kidnapping" with a picture of her from the school's yearbook.

"Why the ..." Kayla grabbed her purse and headed out the door. Talitha, who had spent the night, ran after her, "Wait up," she called as she grabbed her own purse, "You're not going without me!"

"That's one way to get her out of the funk she was in." she told the air.

"I want to talk to the low down, slimy, stinking jackal who printed this asinine article," she announced as she burst into the newspaper office with the offensive article in the air.

A smartly dressed woman came from behind the front desk and spoke in a soft voice in an attempt to defuse the situation. This was not the first time she had encountered an irate reader of their daily news. "I'll be happy to help you if you would explain what article you are upset about."

Kayla and Talitha ignored the hand the woman held out to them in greeting. "I'm Lilly..."

"Kayla, you don't use that kind of language," Talitha looked at her with surprise.

"Well, I'm learning how, and with idiots like this one I'm going to be an expert real fast!"

"Get that low-down scumbag, poor excuse for a reporter out here! Where is he? Is he such a coward he's hiding behind some woman's skirt?" She was not looking at Lilly, the woman manning the office. She was speaking to the closed door.

"And you can tell your boss he's looking toward having a libel suit on his hands," she turned and told the woman.

She tried again to introduce herself with a sly smile, "I'm Lilly White."

Most of the time this got a laugh and the situation became less threatening. But Kayla was not hearing it. She had a mad on and intended to hold on to it. She demanded to see the reporter.

"You need to calm down or I'll have to call the police," she warned. This was plan B on her list of how to handle disgruntle clients.

"You go right ahead," Kayla answered, "I'm mad enough to take them both on!"

The door opened and Kayla gulped when she looked into deep blue eyes. She could swear they sparkled as the owner of the eyes grinned. His deep voice matched the blue eyes, "I'm Jackal. Better known as Scumbag," he held out his hand in greeting. "And you are?"

Kayla caught herself before she said, "doomed". She straightened her spine and answered with feigned confidence, "The one who's going to pin your hide to the wall! How can you get away with printing stories you dream up? No one has accused me of anything. But why argue over semantics? You jump right over protocol. You probably write lies in a man's obituary before he even bothers to die. I want a retraction right now!" She almost poked him in the chest then thought better of it. *"It's probably solid as a rock."*

"And the next time find a decent picture of me," she flung at him as she marched out.

"Next time?" grinned Talitha as she bit down on her double decker sandwich.

They were still laughing at her last comment to Nathanael Harbinger as they munched on lunch at the outdoor café, "Yeah the first two pictures weren't that great."

"If he prints a retraction it'll probably be on the back page in small print."

"Did that woman say her name was Lilly White?" Kayla roared with laughter as it suddenly dawned on her.

CHAPTER 9

KAYLA TO BE QUESTIONED

"Nathanael, my office **Now!**" the order came from his boss. "I heard the exchange that went on in the lobby. Did you know for a fact that Miss Adair has been accused of kidnapping as we printed in our today's paper?"

"She really did pitch a fit didn't she? Some spitfire she is."

"**Mr. Harbinger!**"

"Well no. But my source swore to me it would happen today. I've never found my source to be wrong before. And I did see a woman from CPS take the child."

"So did you bother to check this rumor out before you submitted the piece?"

"Actually I didn't have time to follow through. But I did see the woman take a child who was not Miss Adair's from the house."

"Did you check it out?"

"Well a woman there asked to see an ID and her credentials showed she was indeed from CPS. I did ask a neighbor who told me Kayla didn't have children. And as I said the script was ready to roll. Tomorrow would have been too late. I wanted us to have the scoop before everyone else."

"Do you realize we have a responsibility to the public to print only true facts? We are not one of those tabloids that print anything true or not just to sell a few papers. We are in the news business to inform our readers, to print facts not dream up stories. Our reputation is at stake here. We've been fielding calls about Miss Adair all morning thanks to your article. You have been one of our best reporters until now. I don't know what I'm going to do about it. But as of today you are on leave."

"I wonder what her motive is. Everybody has a motive. My instincts tell me there is a story tied to this. And I'm the one who's going to get to the bottom of it," Nathanael mumbled to himself. But Lilly White's ears tuned in.

Danny slapped the newspaper on the table, "She's already being charged for kidnapping. It wasn't supposed to work that way. All our plans just went down the drain. All that work for nothing. Now what do we do?"

Becky glared at Danny, "Yeah what do we do now? All your big plans to get some big money just blew up in your face along with your promises to me. I **am** an idiot as you so frequently call me. I'm an idiot for listening to you."

"I still have a trick or two left," Danny mumbled as he thought of his former cell mate who had bragged about his ability to hack into anyone's computer.

"This is interesting," Chief White muttered as he laid his breakfast of sausage and egg biscuit on his desk. He folded the daily news to the headlines, leaned back in his swivel desk chair, and put his hands behind his head with his fingers laced as he pondered the news item.

"Do you know anything about a kidnapping at the mall last week?" he called out to his deputy who was in his office next door. He had a feeling that what started out to be a good day was beginning to turn in another direction.

Deputy Black walked to Chief White's office and leaned against the door frame, "The only action I know about at the mall was the pseudo heist last Friday. You know I called you about the two small-time crooks who tried to walk out with a beaded purse. I told you I thought I recognized one of them from some wanted poster. They were just a little too edgy for just a simple shoplifting. I thought something else was up with those two. And you told me to lay low and see what else happened."

"Don't you work security at the mall? This news item states a kidnapping took place there. Why weren't you called to investigate if it was a kidnapping?" the chief's chair snapped back in the upright position.

"Let me see that paper," the deputy walked into the office and took the paper from the chief's hands, "Would you believe it happened at the same store, Sophisticates?"

"That's what I've been trying to tell you. Why weren't you informed?" the chief's voice raised a decimal.

"Wait now. Let me think." He put one hand under his arm pit and rested his chin on his other hand as he pondered "I did hear something over the intercom about a child being found. I was busy at the time with the shoplifters. So I didn't check it out. But it did strike me as odd that they were looking for a child's lost parent instead of a parent looking for a lost child. The last I heard Security was asking for her parents to come to the front desk."

"But why weren't we called if there was a kidnapping? Kidnapping is a federal offence! It doesn't come under mall security authority. I'm going over to the newspaper office right now to find out what this is all about!" Chief White, the chief of police, snatched the paper from his deputy's hand and stomped out.

"I wasn't called because a child being found is not a kidnapping," he told the empty space. His boss had left.

The chief rushed out of his office, weaved his way through a crowd of people in the hall, and passed a crowd standing in front of the police department. He drove to the Daily News and shouldered his way in using his badge as a pass. A line of people stood in the front doorway and spilled out into the parking lot.

"I want to talk with Mr. Harbinger," he demanded of the receptionist Miss White.

"Well take a number and get in line," She said sarcastically as she pointed to the crowd, "As you can see there are a few other people waiting for the same thing."

"They are all waiting to speak with Mr. Harbinger?" he looked around in surprise.

"Yep, every last one of them. We can't get anything done because of the raucous. The phones have been ringing all morning. Our computers are filled with e-mails. Everybody wants a piece of Mr. Harbinger or Miss Adair. Parents are worried about their children. Townspeople are clamoring for justice to be served."

"So that's why I had to fight my way out of my own office at the police station." The fact just hit him. He had been so determined on reaching the writer of the offending article he had not noticed the crowd.

The crowd had been yelling at him but he didn't hear what they were saying. He was too intent on getting to the reporter to find out why a crime had been reported to the news media instead of the proper authorities.

The director of communications came out to meet the chief. "I'm sorry but Nathanael is not available but since I am in charge of the news department I am the responsible party. I would be glad to discuss the problem."

"Well make him available! I want to talk with Mr. Harbinger! What do you mean you would be glad to discuss the problem? I don't discuss the law I enforce it. Do you realize you could be charged with withholding criminal evidence if your newsman is correct?"

"A retraction is being printed at this moment."

"Retraction? A retraction will not erase the damage already done. The general public has been informed that a trusted teacher has been charged with kidnapping! But we who are in charge of law enforcement have not charged her for any crime. We don't even have reason to believe a crime has been committed. No one has reported a kidnapping! No one has filed a missing person report. Now if Mr. Harbinger isn't here, I'll be on my way. And I'll check to see if we need to bring charges against you for breaking the law."

Chief White went back to his office and addressed the crowd. "The news media printed an erroneous item," He explained, "It has no merit. There has been no arrest."

Then he went in and ordered his deputy to go out and find Nathanael Harbinger and bring him in for questioning even if he has to doing so with him **screaming and kicking**.

Lilly called Nathanael on his cell phone to warn him that the chief of police had been there demanding to talk with him. "Miss Adair isn't the only one who is not very happy about your article. The chief was livid. He accused you of committing a crime. He too threatened to sue."

"Thanks for the heads up Lilly," Nathanael said as he headed toward the police station to get the confrontation over with.

"Nathanael you have some explaining to do. I want you to tell me why I should not arrest you right now for withholding facts about a crime. Or did you make up that article? Why shouldn't I put you in jail for inciting two riots, one at my office and another at your place of employment? Why are you not being sued by Miss Adair for defamation of character?"

Chief White pointed his finger in his face, "Where do you get your information?"

"I followed the emergency vehicle and your police unit to her home. I saw a social worker take a child from the home. I did my homework and found out that Miss Adair does not have a child. Even though the child did insist that Miss Adair is her mother. My inquiries show she isn't the child's mother. Her fellow teachers know nothing about a child. Miss Adair herself denies having a child. The security guard confirms that Miss Adair said she was not the child's mother. She was seen leaving the mall with a child, a child that is not hers to take. Isn't that considered kidnapping?"

"I am not fond of ambulance chasers to start with. But I put up with you news reporters because as you say 'the public has a right to know'. But for you to assume a crime has been committed and spread it across the news is criminal. Just because you see a woman being placed into an ambulance doesn't give you the right to print that she has committed a crime. My deputy was there, remember? Did you see him charge her with a crime?"

On his way home Nathanael got a text from Lilly, "If I were you I'd lay low for a while. A man named Gabe came looking for you. He was out for blood, **yours**."

After Mr. Harbinger was allowed to leave, Deputy Black asked his boss, "Chief weren't you a little rough on him? Didn't you say you were going to look into the matter yourself even though the rookie's report of the emergency stated 'A hysterical Miss Adair was transported to the hospital'?"

"Yes but I don't like it when a bulldog gets in the way of an investigation, especially before it becomes an investigation. We have to follow procedure but this news man goes on to print his story without verifying his information. I thought he needed a dose of his own medicine."

"Yeah I could tell you were a little P.O. ed at him."

"Well Deputy, if I'm P O ed why don't **you** to check it out and see what you can find,"

"I talked with the supervisor at Social Services." Deputy Black reported back. "She said the department's first concern was to make sure the child was safe.

"I viewed the tapes, talked with the clerk and the mall security guard. My investigation disclosed these facts. According to the security cameras, store clerks, and lastly Mall security, a woman, Kayla Adair, was shopping in a boutique named Sophisticates. She tried on a formal dress. Then went to another department and browsed through the dress section there. A child walked up to Miss Adair and took her hand. Miss Adair went to a clerk to report a lost child, or a found child would be the better phrase. The search for a lost parent continued far into the night. Miss Adair stayed with the child the entire time. The child kept calling her Mommy. When the mall security guard reached for the child's hand she, the child, responded in a fearful manner. The tapes showed the child clinging to Kayla. The clerk and security guard emphasized the fact that Kayla clearly did all she could in the search for a parent.

"The security guard tried to find the real mother. No one came forward so she had no choice. She knew she could get into trouble if she didn't notify someone in authority when a child is involved. Therefore, she called social services the next day. She didn't want to because the child was obviously attached to Kayla and did not want to be separated from her. She became quite upset when Ms. Brown tried to take charge of her. But Ms. Brown was duty bound to report a child had been found.

The deputy finished the story, "So social services did their duty even though the child insisted that Kayla was her mother. They took the child into protective custody. If those are the facts, Chief, what did Miss Adair do that was so wrong?"

"The only problem is Miss Adair carried the child home with her instead of turning her over to Social Services."

"But it was very late and the child kept calling Miss Adair Mommy. From my investigation the child seemed to be afraid of the security guard. She was clinging to Miss Adair. Would you have turned the child in? Would you have called Social Services to come get the child that late at night? Wouldn't that be heartless?"

Chief White shrugged his shoulders, "Sometimes following the law stinks."

"Okay what do we do now Chief?"

"We need to talk with Miss Adair. The question is how do we go about it without the newshound picking up the scent again? Should we go to her home? Should we bring her in?"

CHAPTER 10

GABE COMFORTS KAYLA

Gabe was apprehensive when he arrived at Kayla's house. He didn't know exactly what to do. Kayla was his friend. Yet they were more than just friends. They were comrades, buddies, pals. She was one of his best friends. They had been going out every Friday night for several years. Then last Friday she was not at home when he went by to pick her up. She had not called to cancel. She was just not home. That wasn't like Kayla. She had always been very dependable. She knew he had planned a special night. He had told her about a new restaurant and wanted to go there.

"Great!" She had exclaimed, "I've wanted to go check out that new boutique at the mall. Now I have a good excuse."

"She seemed pleased when I told her it was a chic establishment." Gabe told himself as he stood at the door.

He hesitated. "Should I ring her doorbell? What if she doesn't want to see me? But those pictures in the papers are disturbing. She had her picture plastered on the front page two days in a row. The story about her being a kidnapper can't be right. That's just not like Kayla."

"What can I say, 'Hey I saw you in the papers'?"

He gasped when she opened the door. He didn't say a thing. He just took her in his arms and held her. She was in terrible shape. She was still in her pajamas even though it was well after nine. Her hair was in tangles. He could tell she was suffering from the lack of sleep because of the black circles under her eyes.

"Aw Sweetheart, I'm so sorry," he sympathized as he led her to the sofa and wrapped her in his arms.

She leaned on his chest and started to cry. There were multiple reasons why she was crying. She was angry. She was crying from the lack of sleep. She was crying from worry. She was crying because she was confused. She was crying because she was sorry. She was crying because God didn't seem to be listening to her prayers for help.

Most of all she was angry. That was one of the things she hated about herself. When she got angry she could not defend herself because she started to cry. How could anyone take her serious when she's crying like a baby? Crying made her furious and that would cause her to cry even harder.

She was angry about the whole situation. She was angry because someone left an innocent child at the mall. She was angry because some mean-spirited reporter printed a false story about her being arrested. But what was worse he printed terrible pictures of her in the paper. She was angry about the threatening letter. What did that threatening letter have to do with anything?

She was crying from the lack of sleep. Her nerves were already shot and the lack of sleep didn't help. She was worried about Sandy even though she was not her responsibility. She was scared for Sandy. What would happen to her?

She was confused about the whole situation. Why did the child come to her? And why did she insist Kayla was her mother? Did God send Sandy her way? If so why?

She was sorry that she had not contacted Gabe again after she left the message. She should have followed up with another call. He deserved that much after she stood him up even though she had been distracted by the circumstances.

So here she was with her arms around Gabe's neck wetting his shirt with her torrent of tears. Gabe was a willing participant. He was glad he could be of comfort to his good friend. They sat in silence until Kayla was spent, the crying gig over.

"Okay the pity party is over. I feel much better. You're not only a good friend but a good sport as well." She patted him on the chest as she got up from the sofa.

"So why don't I fix us some lunch?" Kayla said in a perky voice and started toward the kitchen.

"I have a better idea," Gabe answered as he followed.

She crossed the foyer which was between the den and kitchen and stopped short and stood in shock at the sight. The mirror in the foyer showed how bedraggled she looked.

"Oh for goodness sake Gabe why didn't you tell me?"

"Why don't you get dressed and I'll take you out for lunch? You owe me a dinner date anyway."

"I'm really sorry about that. I know you made reservations but I got a little distracted that day."

"Don't worry about it. I can always make another reservation. I still intend to take you there. But right now a nice lunch at our favorite diner sounds good to me. Now go get presentable."

"That may take some time," Kayla remarked as she spied herself again in the mirror.

Then she got another shock as she glanced out the small window beside the front door. Two uniformed men were walking toward the front door.

"Miss Adair," the chief addressed Kayla as she and Gabe stood in the doorway. "We need to talk with you at the station. Would you come with us please?"

"Not until she has had a chance to change," Gabe spoke in her behalf.

"And you are?" asked Chief White.

"A friend who saw the pictures some reporter printed of her in the daily news. Her image in her night clothes has already been plastered on the front page. Can't you at least give her a chance to change?"

The two policemen did remember the pictures. The man was right; she did deserve a chance to freshen up. They weren't going to charge her with anything anyway; they just wanted to talk with her.

"Okay why don't you come down around one o'clock? That should give you sufficient time to do whatever you need to do."

"Thank you, I'll be there at one," Kayla was relieved. She definitely didn't want to go to the station in the shape she was in.

"You go get ready. I'm going to call a lawyer friend and ask him to meet us at the station. They may not like it if you lawyer up but it's just as a precaution. It's better to err on the side of caution."

The young wannabe reporter Nathanael had hired to watch Kayla's house relayed the news to him. He also stopped by the newspaper to submit a news item 'the police had visited Kayla'. He hoped this would get his foot in the door for a job as news collector at the Daily News. It appeared that even though the Nathanael's report about Kayla was premature it was close to the truth. So Nathanael Harbinger was reinstated as a journalist at the Daily News.

"I knew it. Something is going on and I intend to be the one to get the whole story." Nathanael muttered as he strutted through the lobby and stopped at Lilly's desk, "Lilly you are my right-hand man uh I mean woman. I can always count on you to keep me up on the latest. Thanks." He knew a little flattery would keep her on his side.

Lilly blushed as he walked out the door. Yes, she was on his side.

Kayla and Gabe arrived at the police station at one o'clock as promised. But the entire area was in the midst of chaos. The shrill deafening scream of sirens vibrated throughout the complex. Heavily armed Police were scrambling to their vehicles. From what they could decipher, something had happened at O'Malley's Construction Company, the most respected company in the city. Dealing with the emergency took precedence over everything else. When a woman manning the front desk finally noticed Kayla and Gabe were there, she barely took time to tell them to go home. "We don't have time to deal with you right now," she told them.

CHAPTER 11

GUARD SHOT

Sirens could be heard a mile away as the police sped to the crime scene. A guard at O'Malley's Construction Company had been shot. The 911 call came in just after noon. The entire police force scrambled to their feet. Only a few were left to man the station.

Law enforcement wasn't the only group that scrambled to get to the scene. The news media was on the way. This was big news. Something had happened at the largest place of business around. It was a landmark. It represented the beginning of the beloved city. It was owned by Arthur O'Malley. He was the third generation to run the company. The O'Malley family had started the construction business when the town was about to crumble into dust.

At one time textiles were the main source of employment. The owners of the textile mills had made a fortune, but then moved their companies overseas looking for cheap labor. The people began to lose hope as businesses closed one after another. Shoppers that had previously filled the streets were gone. It was as if they just faded away and disappeared into the boardwalk. All that was left were ghosts.

Those who stayed were resilient hard working people who were willing to work an honest day's labor for an honest day's pay. Unwilling to let the town die they called town meetings. Committees were formed to carry out various activities. A committee was created to go in search of companies willing to invest in the people. Renovations began. They started repairing old buildings and building new ones in the place where old ones had fallen. The streets and sidewalks were spruced up. These activities in themselves caused the people to have a brighter outlook on life. The first building to get a new face was the church. They began to have a spirit of hope and faith. The spirit was catching. Some that had packed up ready to leave decided to stay.

The name New Town no longer seemed to fit. The sign with that name was replaced with a large sign announcing, "Welcome to the town of Live Oak" in bright colorful lettering. A picture of a tall oak tree with wide branches and deep roots was painted on the large sign. This depicted the spirit of the community. Their roots were here and they intended to stay. The whole town was in attendance to see the new sign installed. Just after the inauguration a celebration of the new born town was held in the new community center.

It was as if a miracle happened. Arthur O'Malley's great grandfather saw the advertisement sent out by the search committee. He decided to visit this new town. What he saw was the potential. He saw hardworking people, people of faith, people who were full of hope and willing to act on that hope. He saw a town with people who had been down but refused to give up. Instead they worked to rebuild, repaint, clean up and advertise for help. That spirit caused O'Malley to decide to base his construction company there.

That's why the O'Malley family was so well thought of. The O'Malley Company meant more to the town than a place to work. As the company grew so did the town. It was now a thriving city. It now sported many manufacturing companies. Small towns and communities began to spring up around. O'Malley himself was one on the pillows of the community. Not only did he supply much needed jobs for many, he worked to help secure housing for the less fortunate. He was one of deep faith and held different positions in the church. The entire area seemed to depend upon this trusted company one way or another.

But unfortunately along with progress comes an undesirable element. That's what happened to one of O'Malley's employees. He was shot down as he performed his duties.

EMS vehicles as well as the news media were already on the way.

Security had shut down the whole place. No one was allowed to enter or leave the premises. Knowing the media would be splashing the news across the city, many of the company employees had already used cell phones to contact family members to let them know they were all right.

Upon arrival the police found the work place in a frenzied state. A security guard had been shot. He was lying just inside the main office doorway. Someone had entered the main office during lunchtime and robbed the two women who were in the process of preparing the employees' payrolls. The women were found locked in a closet like vault. In order to get a clear unblemished account of the robbery the two women were questioned right after they were released from the closet. A forensics expert was called to the scene as soon as the call came in that someone had been shot.

The police immediately sent out teams scouring the premises looking for anything which could be connected to the crime. Another team began questioning anyone who may have pertinent information. Squads from West Side station were asked to come and help with the investigation since there were so many people to question.

There was another problem. This was the week of spring break for schools. Some of the regulars had been replaced with temps for the week. This was the case of the security guard as well as the front gate guard. They were new on the job and it would have been impossible to scrutinize everyone especially during shift change. Those entering the premises were checked closely. They did check each one entering the gates and all had proper IDs. The regulars would have recognized a new face coming in and would have double checked the credentials.

The service entrances were on the other side of the company complex. Suppliers and their representatives entering the service entrances were closely monitored. No one was allowed on the grounds without proper identification.

So the perpetrator had to be one of the employees or someone who entered using a false ID.

Approximately two hundred thousand dollars had been stolen. One good thing to count on, since the bills had been supplied by a bank, the Serial Numbers were sequential. In his haste the robber had dropped a bundle as he fled. An APB went out to businesses especially banks to be on the lookout for bills carrying any of the serial numbers. If any of the money was spent in one place, there would be a good chance it would be traced to the robber. If he tried to deposit the cash, banks could spot it quickly.

The investigators wanted to get an account from everyone in the plant while the incident was fresh in their mind. So they asked them to stay for questioning. Before the news spread causing alarm among the community, each employee was asked to contact a member of his or her family to let them know they were okay.

The employees were divided into groups according to sections of the plant they worked. Each group was then taken to conference rooms for further questioning. Those who worked close to the scene and the gate guards were questioned individually.

No one had noticed a stranger on the grounds. All the people who entered had IDs. All vehicles checked out. Security cameras were scrutinized with no results.

The only ones directly involved in the incident were the two women doing payroll and the guard who had received the distress call from the now dead guard.

The two women were questioned independently. Their account of the incident was pretty much the same.

Chief White took out a tape recorder and placed it in front of Mrs. Gray, the cashier, "I want you to tell me what happened. Just start telling me off the top of your head. Don't try to reason anything out. That way we may get a clearer picture. After that we'll go back and fill in empty spaces and try to refine details."

"We were in the back of the office near the safe which was open. Oh yes, the office door was locked. We are always careful to make sure the office is locked when we do payroll. I was counting out the cash for each employee and Goldie, uh Mrs. Golden, was keeping account of each transaction. My mind was intent on making sure we made no mistakes. My back was toward the door but I saw shock on Goldie's face and heard a man's voice at the same time. 'Ladies', he said in a calm voice. Then he said something about helping us out and to put the money in a briefcase. Then he locked us in the closet. After he closed the door I heard the guard yell "Halt" and a loud pop."

Deputy Black interviewed Mrs. Golden, the bookkeeper, "I'm going to tape the conversation so we'll have your initial reaction to the incident. I want you to start with where you were and what you were doing just before the robbery. Then tell me as much as you can about what happened after that. Then if necessary I will ask questions to clear up some details."

"We ate our lunch in the break room at eleven as we always do on Thursday," Mrs. Golden began as she thought back. "Then we went into the office where the vault is. We were in the process of preparing the salaries when the thief opened the door and walked in. I may have heard a click but my mind was on the count."

"Now how did he do that? We always lock it before we began," she said to herself as an afterthought.

"Don't worry about it. Just tell what you remember as it comes to you. We can analyze and decipher later."

Mrs. Golden continued, "He walked into the office, pulled out a gun, and announced, 'I'm going to relieve you of this tedious job of counting out the salaries.' He opened the briefcase and told me, 'If you would be kind enough to place the money in here I'll be out of your way, after I lock you in the closet that is.' As soon as the vault was closed I heard the security guard yelling for backup on his radio. Then I heard a shot and thud. That must have been the guard falling. Backup security was there within minutes. We stayed in the vault until it was opened by them because we were afraid the gunman was still out there".

Testimony from the guard who received the call added little to the information. The dead guard had yelled into his mike alerting his fellow guards. But he didn't wait for backup.

As soon as the guard got the call he had sent an 'all-men-aboard alert' but they all were along the fenced perimeter of the grounds. They were there because there had been sightings of young teens in the surrounding area and there were concerns that one of them may get hurt trying to scale the fence.

Police tried desperately to piece together the few facts they had on the robbery and murder. Weeks passed and they were no closer to solving the murder. They seemed to be getting nowhere with the investigation. None of the money had been used. The weapon had not been found. None of the leads panned out.

CHAPTER 12

RETURN TO KIDNAPPING CASE

The investigation on the murder and robbery at O'Malley Construction Company was at a stand-still. Mrs. Golden and Mrs. Gray were the only eye witnesses. Several who fit the description were picked up and questioned but each one failed to pan out. Leads coming in were checked out but there was not enough evidence to hold anyone. It was so frustrating they had a hard time dealing with it.

Chief White called a meeting to evaluate the situation, "We seem to be getting nowhere with the investigation. We know most of the people who work at the company. Maybe we're so closely connected to this company and its employees it could be clouding our judgement. We're trying so hard to solve the case we may be missing something in our diligence. We need to step back and view the case from another perspective."

He thought concentrating on other cases may clear their minds. After that they would begin again with a fresh start, "Besides that we've been letting other cases slide."

So, he decided to split them into several teams. The top notch investigative squad was assigned to continue the O'Malley case. They were to look at all angles, check out all venues, resort the information into several different categories, and try a new viewpoint. They were to review old crimes and check with other counties to see if any matched the M.O.

Chief White went back to pending cases, "I hate to have a lot of loose ends hanging over my head," he told his officers, "We let a few things slip while we worked on the O'Malley robbery and murder. Let's see what we can do to clear these up." He placed his hand on a stack of files on his desk.

One case was particularly odd, the investigation of the found child. He took out the nearly empty folder and reviewed the information. "Nothing much here but it needs to be cleared up and closed," he told himself. Then spoke on the intercom, "Mike I need to see you and Erica in my office."

Chief White didn't think there was much to solve, an open and closed case so to speak. So he assigned the investigation to one of his regular officers, Mike Core and the rookie, Erica. Mike wasn't too happy about the assignment. It seemed to be a trivial case and he didn't like being given trivial cases. He wanted to be in on the big ones. He felt his training as an investigator was overlooked. He wanted to be on the O'Malley case. Instead he was given this mundane case and saddled with a rookie as well.

Mike went back to his desk and frowned at the folder he had just been handed and passed it on to Erica Key his rookie trainee. "See what you can find out about this," he told her as he walked out.

As she previewed the files in the folder she noticed an interesting note. A reporter at Daily News had overstepped his role by publishing an article about Kayla Adair being a kidnapper. So, she decided to start by visiting the reporter at the Daily News. As she entered through the sliding glass doors she noticed the receptionist at her desk. Lilly smiled as she greeted Erica but there was a slight change in her smile when Erica asked to speak with Nathanael. Erica, who was very perceptive when it came to reading people's body language, noticed the change in Lilly's tone when she asked to speak with Mr. Harbinger.

"I wonder what that was about." She asked herself as she was shown to the office. She took one look at the imposing Nathanael and understood, "The old green eyed monster must have raised his head."

Erica's visit with Nathanael was almost fruitless. He told her his side of the story. "I heard the call on my scanner and followed the EMS and police to Kayla's home. Two women took a child from the house as Kayla was loaded into the ambulance. A woman who identified herself to Talitha showed up and protested the taking of the crying, screaming child. That's when the woman who held the child said she was from child protection service. That gave me an indication something was amiss. So, I followed up by talking with Kayla's fellow teachers. They told me she didn't have a child. Then I heard about the incident at the mall involving a found child and Kayla carried her home with her."

"What about the picture you took of Kayla?"

"Oh yes, I took pictures. I'm a reporter. That's what I do. I take pictures and gather information."

"What about the next day? You called Kayla a kidnapper in your article."

"Well Kayla doesn't have a child. She went to the mall without a child but carried one home with her when she left. Wouldn't you call it kidnapping?"

Erica determined that Mr. Harbinger had expounded on what he saw and made assumptions about what he heard through the grapevine. The article printed in the paper was not based on facts. It was pure speculation on his part. She was a policewoman. Police deal with facts and it was a fact an unattractive picture of a woman whose hair and clothes were matted with syrup was printed in the daily news. Then the next day an article appeared in the news calling Kayla a kidnapper. Erica felt Nathanael had indeed overstepped his role as reporter of news.

Nathanael's interest in Kayla's situation was rekindled by the visit from Erica. "There must be something going on there." He thought for a minute or two and then went out to speak with Lilly, "Have you ever gone shopping at the mall at a boutique called Sophisticates?"

"Yes, well I have been there but I didn't buy anything. It carries quite a line of dressy evening wear which is out of my budget range. Why?"

"I want you to scout out the place and check on a story I'm working on. I would go myself but I've already done that. They already know me; I can't just wander in as if I were a shopper."

Lilly was thrilled to be asked by Nathanael for help. That meant she had been noticed after all, "I would love to help you," she cooed a little too sweetly for his comfort. He needed her help so he pretended innocence.

"I think a woman shopper could get more information by just casually talking about an incident that happened there. I know how women like to gossip."

She was happy to help but she was not too happy about the last comment. But she let it go because she really wanted to please. That being the case, she went to the mall and pretended to shop. She thought about how nice it would be if Nathanael gave her a reason to buy a fancy dress.

When she finished the chore she had very little new information. The woman had indeed carried a child home with her. But it had been very late in the night and the manager of Sophisticates had been impressed with the way Kayla handled the situation. The woman in charge of security at the mall had run a check on Kayla. All evidence indicated the child would be perfectly safe with Kayla. The child had persisted in her claim that Kayla was her mother. Kayla had tried every avenue to find the mother or person who brought her to the mall. No one in security wanted to shuttle the child off to child protection services that late at night. That's why Kayla carried the sleeping child home with her. Lilly had to admit she wanted to find at least one kink in Kayla's armor but she didn't.

When she reported back to Nathanael his response was, "No one is that clean. She must have something hidden in her background."

"And I intend to find it," he mumbled to himself.

Since her sidekick aka trainer had dropped the 'found child' investigation into her lap and disappeared, Erica decided go it alone to interview the other agencies involved: EMS, School, Mall security, her own Police department, and child protection services.

She started out by contacting EMS. Their records showed that a 911call came from a security guard at the mall. The guard reported she heard screams when she called to check on Kayla and the child. They dispatched a unit and found the pajama clad, crying, incoherent Kayla sitting in a pile of pancakes and syrup. They transported her to the hospital. The interview with EMS ended there.

She went to the mall to talk with the person who placed the 911 call. After explaining she was doing a follow up investigation into the 'found child case' she was directed to the security office.

"I called to check on the child," Marge began, "The call was answered but before I could get a word in I heard a woman scream followed by a child's scream. I told the person on the phone to hold on because I was calling for help. After I placed the 911 call I tried to call Kayla back but the phone was busy. I raced to Kayla's house to check on her and the child. I arrived just as a protesting Kayla was being loaded into the emergency vehicle. It was a mad house there. Two women were taking the screaming child as another woman questioned their actions. A news reporter was taking pictures and asking questions which were being ignored. The neighbors had congregated in their yards and others were out in the street watching. I didn't get a chance to find out what was going on."

"Why were you calling to check on a child who was not lost?"

"The child was found at the mall on my watch. Kayla and I were involved in trying to find the mother. Aren't you doing the same thing?" she asked Erica.

"Actually, I was checking on the 911 call that involved a woman and an erroneous article in the news. I found out from EMS you were the one who placed the 911 call. Somewhere along the line a child and child protection services got involved. It seems I may have started my investigation in the middle instead of at the beginning."

"That must be why it's beginning to be quite confusing. After I interview everyone on my list, I'll have to go back and try to put the pieces together in order," she made a mental note to herself.

"So why don't you start by telling me where you become involved?"

Marge looked at her watch, "It's time for my shift to end. I see my replacement coming in now. Why don't we discuss this over dinner?"

"Dinner sounds great to me. I was too busy to eat lunch so I'm starved." Erica took her purse off the back of the chair, slung it over her shoulder, and followed Marge out the door.

When they entered the restaurant Erica was surprised to see Mike there. From the evidence in front of him he had been there for a while. *"So this is where he's been hiding out,"* she thought to herself.

"Mike," she acknowledged him as they passed by on the way to be seated.

Erica forgot all about Mike as Marge related her side of the story as they ate. "I have already told this to Chief White. I was called by the manager of Sophisticates to help find the parent or parents of a child that had been found," Marge began, "I met a woman, Kayla, who had found the child. Actually according to Kayla the child found her. She was casually browsing in the boutique when the child came up to her and called her 'Mommy'. We announced over the speakers that a child had been found. No one came to claim her. My staff got involved by going to each store in the mall trying to find the person who brought the child in. By the time the stores closed we had not found anyone who knew anything about the child. Every time we asked the child about her mother she insisted that Kayla was her mother. We reviewed the tapes from surveillance cameras and found nothing of importance. We didn't even have a clip showing the child entering the mall."

"You said she insisted that Kayla was her mother. Did she call you or any of the other women Mommy?"

"No, as a matter of fact she held on to Kayla and would not let anyone else hold her hand. She was especially leery of me. She did talk to Miss Sommer, Rene', the manager of the boutique. But she shied away from me when I approached her. She balked when I tried to get her to go with me to my office."

"Who made the decision to let her go home with Kayla?"

"It must have been an unspoken mutual agreement. It became very late, around midnight. We were all exhausted from the futile search. The child was asleep in Kayla's arms. Because she would not allow anyone else to hold her, Kayla offered to carry the child home with her. We didn't object. It seemed to be the only solution at the time."

Did you know Kayla before that night?"

"No."

"Weren't you concerned about allowing the child to go home with someone you had never met before?"

"I forgot to mention I had a coworker run a check on her while we were searching. There was nothing to indicate it would be a problem."

Erica looked up and saw Mike. He seemed to stand out because he was in his policeman's uniform. Then she noticed there were three people in the room in uniform: Marge, Mike, and herself. "Did the child shy away from anyone else at the mall?" she asked.

"Let me think. Yes I think she seemed afraid of the other security officers. Does that mean anything?"

"You and the other security officers were in uniform. Is that right?"

"I am following your chain of thought. You may be on to something. She may be afraid of police or people in uniform."

"After that night did you have any contact with either of them?"

"Yes, the next day Mrs. Goodman and I visited Kayla. My supervisor, Mrs. Goodman, was concerned about protocol and wanted to check on the child. That was an interesting visit. The way the child handled our interview was quite fascinating."

"Wait!" Marge seemed to stop in midsentence, "It just dawned on me and this may go along with your hypothesis. She was hesitant to come into the room when she saw us. Kayla called her and she came running but stopped short when she saw us. She ran over to Kayla and wrapped arms around Kayla's legs. We were wearing our uniforms."

"That is interesting. Okay now what was so fascinating about the interview?"

"After Kayla led her over to a sofa and sat beside her she seemed less frightened of us. I asked what her name was and she answered, 'Sandy'. That was the name Kayla called her because of her hair color. When I asked about her last name she thought we were playing a game that she and Kayla had been playing. I tried playing along. She told me her last name was Adair and she lived 'here with Mommy' and then announced that she no longer wanted to play and left the room. Mrs. Goodman told Kayla that she was duty bound to report the incident to the proper authorities and we left."

"So the next contact was the 911 call?"

"Yes, as you probably have learned by now from the EMS worker. I called Kayla and apparently the screams and crying I heard were coming from Kayla and Sandy. I had no idea what was happening. I hate that Sandy was taken away from Kayla that way. It must be hard on both of them. It appears we have come full circle. That's where your interview began. I hope you have better luck than I in finding her parents."

Erica closed the recorder and stood to leave, "Thanks to you I have more to go on than I found in the first file.

Erica found very little that would help in finding the child's parents from her interviews with the school system. She first contacted the administrator. Who told her Kayla had been a loyal employee for ten years. Just as with all employees a background check had been run on her before being hired. There were no red flags. In Yearly teacher evaluations she was always given a positive report.

Because spring break had begun Erica decided to contact Kayla's fellow teachers by phone. She would follow up with a visit if she got a hint that further investigation was warranted. She found nothing significant from most teachers except they had already been contacted by a nosy news reporter. The information was inconclusive. Kayla was a likeable person and as far as they knew did not have a child. One teacher, Gabe, was upset that Erica was investigating Kayla instead of trying to find Sandy's parents. "Gabe Elder seems to be protective but no need to follow up at this time," she noted in the recorder as she returned to the police station.

It was time to type up her notes of the day and turn them over to Mike her senior partner. It was his duty to report the day's activities to the chief. The day had been long and she was tired. She intended to head home as soon as she finished the day's report. As she entered the station she saw Officer Black at his desk and decided to get one more interview over with.

Officer Black's answers were factual and to the point, "Officer Day responded to the 911 call. In his report he stated a woman, Kayla, was transported to the hospital. Two women from child protective services were there and took a child from the home for 'safe keeping' they said. One woman protested the taking of the child until they showed her their ID. A news hound kept getting in the way. Neighbors as usual were out to see what was going on. A woman who worked security at the mall showed up. She said she had made the 911 call. Child protective services had taken the child and a distraught woman was on the way to the hospital. That was the extent of the report so I assumed the emergency had been taken care of.

"But the next day a picture of a disheveled Kayla showed up on the front page of the newspaper. The following day another picture of her showed up in the news with the caption 'Teacher Kidnapper'. That's when our department became involved. To say our chief was angry is putting it mildly. He went to the newspaper office to chew out Mr. Harbinger who wrote the column but he was not there. Somehow he got wind that we were looking for him and came in on his own.

"After he questioned Mr. Harbinger, Chief decided to talk with Miss Adair. We went to her house but she was… Let's just say she was not ready for an outing. She agreed to come by the station on Monday. When she and her friend arrived as promised we had an emergency on our hands. The robbery and murder of a security guard at O'Malley's Construction Company put a hold on the hypothetical kidnapping.

"Sometimes when mall security is short of help I do a little moonlighting. I later discovered I was there when the child, Sandy, latched on to Kayla. At the time I was already involved in a shoplifting case at the very same boutique. Since I already had my hands full, I did not get involved in the parent search."

"Check on coincidence of two cases at the mall," She made another recorded note.

"This is going to be a doozy of a puzzle to put together. For a simple case this one has changed into one with some weird twists," She told herself. She typed up her report, turned it over to Mike, and headed home.

The next order of business was a trip to child protective services.

With the privacy act in place Erica could not be told much but she got the impression all was not well with the 'found child'. There was a slight hesitation from Mrs. Lattimore when Erica asked how Sandy was doing. The question was ignored as Mrs. Latimore explained why she was in the hands of CPS.

"We did take the child into protective custody when we went to Miss Adair's home. Miss Adair was being transported to the hospital. Even if she was her mother she couldn't take care of the child. She and the child were both protesting. Miss Adair didn't want to go to the hospital and the child didn't want to go with me."

"Then why did the paramedics take Miss Adair to the hospital against her wishes?"

"It was my call. Probably because I told them she was out of control."

"So they took your word over Miss Adair's protests?" This revelation upset Erica.

"Well, not just my word. There were other indications or reasons to believe me. The caller who made the 911 call reported hearing screams over the phone when she called Miss Adair's home. The door had been slammed in my face just before the screaming. We went in to see what was wrong. Miss Adair and the child were unkempt. They were still in their pajama and covered in syrup."

"Mental note to self: Went into the home without being invited in. door slammed in her face a sure sign she was not welcome"

"Where is Sandy? You do still call her Sandy?" Erica became more concerned when Mrs. Latimore hesitated again. Her uneasiness and body language told Erica something was wrong.

"She is uh fine. I'm not at liberty to tell you where she is."

"Okay, as an officer of the law I am investigating a possible kidnapping. It is my duty to collect as much information as I can before we decide a crime has been committed. I would appreciate any information you are allowed to disclose."

The lack of information was making Erica testy. "I'll try to make it simple. I ask a question and you answer yes or no."

"First question, do you call her Sandy?"

"Yes, but…"

"Second question, have you seen her lately?"

"Yes, but…"

"Third question; how is Sandy?"

"This line of questioning has nothing to do with a kidnapping."

"Okay then this fourth question does. Is Sandy still insisting Kayla is her mother?"

"Yes but …"

"I think my interview is over. Thank you for your help, Mrs. Latimore." Erica cut the recorder off and left.

"Sometimes I hate this job. I wanted to tell Officer Key but Sandy's fear of doctors has nothing to do with kidnapping," Mrs. Latimore mumbled as she reached for the phone to call the foster family to check on Sandy. As was her custom when a child is taken into custody she carried Sandy to the doctor for a checkup. When she saw the doctor, Sandy had wrapped her arms around herself and started shivering. Tears rolled down her face as she begged for her 'Mommy'.

"She's a very unhappy child," the foster parent answered when Mrs. Latimore called. "She doesn't eat much and her sleep is interrupted with nightmares. I'm concerned about her health. I know you just had her checked by a doctor but I'm wondering if I need to carry her back just to be sure."

"Let's hold off for a while," Mrs. Latimore answered remembering the adverse reaction Sandy had toward the doctor.

Kayla was the last one on her Erica's list. She was found at church where she had gone to pray for Sandy and about her own behavior, saying Damn in front of Sandy, calling Nathanael a slimy stinking jackal, slamming the door in the women's faces, and not inviting the preacher's wife in when she called on her.

"Lord I know I can pray anywhere but with all that has happened so far I felt the need to ask for forgiveness at Your house of worship," she began.

When Erica could not find Kayla and no one knew where she may be, she sat down and looked at her notes for clues. After reviewing her notes she asked herself, "After all that has happened to her where would I go if I were in her shoes?"

She found Kayla sitting on a bench in the church's prayer garden.

"I'm Erica," she introduced herself as she sat down beside her.

"I was wondering when you would get around to me. Do you know how Sandy is?"

"I wish I had something to tell you but I really don't know how she is." She didn't say anything about her own apprehension because she didn't want to add to Kayla's worry. But there was a hint of something in the interview with Mrs. Lattimore that piqued her interest.

Erica took out the recorder then decided against it as put it back in her briefcase, "You must know by now my investigation is to see if there is any probable cause to bring you in for questioning for kidnapping. I don't know when it all started but two days after we responded to a 911 call an article in the paper got my chief's attention. The article was about a kidnapping. He was not the least bit happy that a hot shot reporter supposedly knew about a crime and wrote about it before it was reported to the police. It seems the reporter saw child protection service take the child and started snooping around and came up with the kidnapping story. I've been contacting everyone who responded to the 911 call and questioning them about what happened. I know this is unorthodox but off the record tell me your version of that 911 call."

"That was one hell of a day. Excuse me Lord I did it again. I was suffering from the lack of sleep and frustrated by the futile search for Sandy's parents. The day before was Sunday and I totally forgot about my duties at church. The preacher's wife came to check on me and I slammed the door in her face. For these reasons I was already in a foul mood when I got up that morning. Then, excuse my language again but there is no other way to convey what happened, all hell broke loose. I got an extortion letter in the mail demanding half a million dollars. I scared Sandy when

I yelled. I tried to calm her by making pancakes for breakfast. Being in the state I was in it was natural that I jumped when the doorbell rang. I dropped the syrupy pancake down my pajamas. I yelled at the two women I thought were selling something. Then the telephone rang. I went to get a paper towel to wipe my hands and somehow got syrup in my hair. I had just answered the phone when the doorbell rang again. The paper towel was stuck to my hands and the whole roll of towels followed me to the door. By this time I was livid. I lost it."

Kayla's hasty recall of what happened pretty much matched the facts Erica had already gathered. She had talked so fast Erica almost missed it.

"I get the picture. From what I've found from the other interviews I can put the rest of the day together," She rose from the bench to leave. She was ready to wrap up the investigation and leave it to social services to decide what to do about Sandy.

"Back up a minute did you say extortion letter? This is the first I've heard about an extortion letter. That puts a different spin on things."

"Well since that report came out in the paper I just chalked it up to some crazy playing a joke." She failed to mention the other note. "2nd time = jail for sure," it said.

"Before you say anything else I think you need to come down to the precinct for a briefing. Do you mind coming in for questioning?"

"Of course not, I reported in before but a murder-robbery case put that meeting aside."

"Even though you dismissed it as a joke, I think it would be a good idea to bring the extortion letter with you." From the expression on Kayla's face she couldn't help but think there was more to it than she let on.

Erica printed her factual notes and turned them over to Mike. But she made another file titled 'Observations and Gut feelings'. The notes inside the folder read:

1. Extortion letter
2. CPS went into the home without being invited in
3. Door slammed in her face a sure sign she was not welcome
4. CPS hesitated when I asked about the child's condition
5. Gabe Elder seems to be protective of Kayla
6. Check on coincidence of two cases at the mall

She put this and the taped recordings in her desk drawer. She planned to peruse them later to see if she may have inadvertently stumbled upon something important.

Without reading the report, Mike filled out the submission form, signed it, and clipped it on Erica's notes which he placed the folder titled 'Kayla Adair possible kidnapper' and filed it the cabinet of active cases.

"Mike what's your take on the kidnapping case you're investigating?" Chief White smiled knowing he put Mike on the spot. He was meeting with Erica and Mike to discuss the case.

Mike hesitated before answering because he had not previewed Erica's notes, "She uh- I'll let my junior partner answer that. I think Miss Key needs the experience."

Chief White turned to Erica, "I read your report which stated facts as told by each person you interviewed. Now let me try to consolidate your notes. Miss Adair was shopping at Sophisticates when a child came up to her. She reported to customer service and tried to find the child's parent. But the child insisted Kayla was her 'Mommy'. The mall was searched by security and when all avenues were exhausted Miss Adair was allowed to take the child home with her. The next day after being contacted by mall security two women from Child Protection Services showed up at Kayla's house. Kayla was already upset because of a letter. Not knowing who the women were shut the door in their face. At the same time Marge from the mall called Kayla to let her know she had reported the incident to Social Services. Screams overheard on the phone caused Marge to call in an emergency. CPS took the child as Miss Adair was being transported to the hospital. Mr. Harbinger observed this and printed an erroneous article about Miss Adair being a kidnapper. Some people who read the article were upset and started calling the school where she worked, the police station, and the newspaper. So, Miss Key these are your findings but what is your gut feeling, your intuition so to speak?"

"I was beginning to think it was an open and shut case. It seemed to be a case of a kind-hearted woman who unknowingly broke the law by carrying a lost child home with her. The reports that came into the station didn't prove to have any substance. Some parents had read the article in the paper about a teacher kidnapper and were concerned about their children. Another reported seeing a woman fitting Kayla's description trying to hide a child when she went to a store. But it was raining that day so I assumed she was shielding the child from the rain not hiding her. There were a few other rumors which failed to pan out." She paused as if that was all she was going to say but since the chief asked about her gut feeling she decided to continue.

"Then what started out to be just an odd case turned into an unusual one when Miss Adair told me about an extortion letter she received in the mail. Of course the letter could be somebody playing a joke as she suggested. I know I'm new at this but I have a feeling there may be more to the case than we first thought. I also have a feeling all is not well with the child. Nothing was said to that effect; it's just an observation. Mrs. Latimore of CPS was hesitant to answer any questions. Her uneasiness and body language hinted that something was wrong."

CHAPTER 13

$50 BILL

Sally asked Becky to carry her to Bert's Fix It Shop to pick up her Charger where it had been painted Cobalt Blue. She ran her hand over the new paint. She loved it. She had loved everything about the Charger except for what she called 'the gangster style' metallic Black paint.

"It is beautiful," Becky agreed with the unsaid admiration.

But Sally could see the question in Becky's eyes, *"How could she afford a car like this?"*

"When the Charger was brought in I knew I just had to have that car. I made a financial agreement with Fred and agreed to pay as much as I could at a time until I had enough for a down payment. Until then I had to rely on unreliable Old Ugly."

It still seemed like a dream to Sally as she thought back over the whole scene and relayed to Becky the circumstances that led to her owning the car.

"This old pile of junk won't last long," the mechanic had told Sally, "I'll try to get it running but ..."

The Volvo had stopped running right in the middle of the road. She was bemoaning the fact that it was taking so long to raise the down payment. So Fred had let her drive the Charger while the Volvo was in the shop. "Remember it's not your car yet."

"And then it will be headed to Bert's Fix it Shop to be painted Cobalt Blue," Sally had promised herself.

"Fred's Auto," Sally answered the phone.

"I'm calling about a car I was told you have. It's a black charger."

"I'm sorry but I've already bought the car. Well I still have one payment to have enough for the down payment," Sally said without thinking.

"*I shouldn't have told him that,*" she admonished himself.

"I really didn't want to buy it. I was hoping to rent it."

"We do have rentals but as I said I'm buying the Charger. We'd be happy to show you a car comparable to it."

"No I want the Charger. You mentioned you still don't quite own it yet. You still need a little more for down payment."

"Yes but."

"Maybe we can help each other. I could rent it from you. Maybe that will be enough for your down payment."

"I'll have to think about that."

"I really would like to rent the car. I promise it will be just for a couple of hours. I just met this girl who's crazy about Chargers. You know how it is. I really would like to show it to her. Think about it. The rent money I pay you will let you have the car sooner."

"I really do need a car that doesn't break down every day. That Volvo is in the shop more than it on the road. The mechanic told me it had died several months ago but no one bothered to tell it so. His suggestion was to see if I could sell it for scrap." She was talking to herself more than to the man on the phone.

"So does that mean you'll rent it?"

"As soon as I get possession I'm going to have it repainted. If you give me the money to finish the down payment, I'll rent it to you after I have it painted." It didn't take long for Sally to make up her mind about renting out the car. She was sick of Old Ugly.

"No, no, don't do that my friend loves the metallic black."

"But that black has got to go,"

"Okay I tell you what I'll do. I'll give you the rent up front today. Tomorrow morning I'll pick it up. Then in the afternoon I'll deliver it myself to the paint shop. It'll be for only half a day. I'll even deliver the Volvo to Al's Junk Yard for you. That's no place for a woman out there anyway."

"So here I am," she told Becky, "the proud owner of a pretty Cobalt Blue Charger. Well I still owe Fred. But it's mine to drive."

"It is pretty and rides like a dream," Becky agreed with Sally.

"I can't wait to see Danny's eyes pop out of his head when I drive up. I can't wait to tell him that Old Ugly is being crushed to death."

Danny didn't say much when Sally boasted about her car. He was a little jealous and still smarting from the setback of his big get-rich plans.

"I know what we should do," Becky was still in a happy for Sally mood. She wasn't about to let Danny's brooding kill the spirit. "Why don't we go out for a few beers and celebrate?"

Danny's mood changed a little. "Okay you buying?" No way was he going to to turn down free beer.

The wind picked up as they left the house. A dust devil whirled around and whipped a strand of Sally's hair into her eyes. Being blinded by her hair she pressed the keyless clicker for the side doors to open but pressed the trunk button instead.

"What's this?" Danny asked as a piece of paper flew out of the trunk. The wind had picked it up and twirled it around. It slowly swung back and forth as it floated downward and settled on the ground as the dust devil moved on.

"Hey look at this. It's a fifty. My luck has changed. I'm buying."

"Well now whose trunk did it come from?" Sally asked as she placed her hands akimbo.

"Finders keepers," Danny waved the bill in her face. "You coming?" He asked as he opened the car door and got in.

On the way to the bar he told them about the time a friend had used a fifty-dollar bill to pay for an item and the clerk swore it was a twenty. "He got so mad she was about to call the police. He didn't want the police involved so he calmed down and asked her to open the cash drawer to check. She acted as if she thought he was going to rob her. But she did open it and there on the twenties was a fifty."

"Becky don't you have a highlighter in your purse? You should have, you're always marking things. You can't look at a magazine without marking all over it." Danny asked as he reached over the front seat with his hand open.

Becky huffed at his comment but reached into her purse, pulled out the highlighter, and handed it to him.

Danny made a big yellow ring around the 50 on the corner of the bill.

When he paid for the beers Danny told him it was a fifty. The bartender held it up toward the light to check it. Then he took out a special marker to make sure.

"Boy he made a big deal out of that," Danny grumbled as he led the way to a table.

"Well you made a big deal out of it yourself," Becky reminded him.

When they returned home Danny was feeling better about his plan. He might have to modify it a bit but he still had a few tricks up his sleeve. It was time to spring the next trap.

Danny had served time with a computer nerd as a cellmate. He bragged to Danny about his hacking abilities. He knew how to cover his tracks. It wasn't his fault for being caught. It was his buddy in crime who didn't follow all his directions. The next time he would not trust anyone else to delete, clean, and destroy. While Danny talked with him he decided he could use his expertise.

He had researched Kayla's background. That was one reason he knew so much about her. She had been raised in a home for children. While there she had practically raised one of the other children. And just before she left the home she received a modest fund from an estranged aunt's estate.

Danny talked his former cell mate into hacking into Kayla's computer at school where she taught. He planted a log which would appear Kayla had tried to create an identity for Sandy. And it looked like Kayla tried to get Sandy enrolled for the next school year. Danny made his friend think he wanted proof he could really do what he bragged about. But Danny was going to use it to extort money from her.

Now that his luck had changed it was time to put more pressure on His pigeon.

He instructed Sally to deliver a small basket with an apple to Kayla at school. The message was 'C UR E-files' 100(KKKKK).

"This is a surprise. But Danny can be really sweet sometimes," Sally commented to herself as she, dressed in a delivery uniform, went to Kayla's school.

"I'd like to deliver this basket to Miss Adair," she told the secretary.

"Well I ... uh .... Okay just leave it here," was the answer.

"That was odd. I wonder why the secretary looked confused. Oh well I'm just the delivery boy."

CHAPTER 14

LIQUOR STORE ROBBERY

Rodney and Ramon had been riding around all morning.

"Man I'm bored, there's nothing to do around here," Rodney sighed.

"Yeah," Ramon agreed, "and Mom's car is about to run out of gas and I can't get any more I don't have any money."

"I know what you mean. I couldn't even buy a pack of cigarettes if I smoked."

"We need some money."

"Yeah, I know that's the truth."

"There's no way I can get any more out of my mom."

"Yeah the only way to get our hands on any is to steal it."

That's when they decided to rob a store.

What they didn't know was this was Al's city and no one dared do business in his territory without his okay.

"Mom would kill me if we used her car to pull a robbery," Ramon winched just thinking of what his mother would do to him. "I had a hard time getting her to let me have it today."

"Why don't we rent a 'junker'? It shouldn't cost too much. We could always ditch the car in case somebody sees us leave the store."

"Now where are you going to get enough money to rent a car even if it is a junker?"

"Well then let's steal one. Since we're going to rob somebody we may as well steal a car.

As they drove around they spotted Fred's Car Lot. "Let's stop and check it out," Rodney suggested.

"There's a lot of used cars in here but I don't think we could even rent one of his recaps." Ramon lamented.

They got out and pretended to car shop. "Can I help you?" they both jumped as a salesman came up behind them.

"We uh we we're just looking for a cheaper car." Rodney stammered. He looked around and saw there were too many other shoppers and salesmen to even try to steal a car.

"Yeah," Ramon backed away from a car he was looking at, "These cost a lot more than we were planning on paying."

"Why don't you try Bert's Fix It Shop?" the salesman suggested, "Sometimes he gets a car in that's a steal of a deal."

The two looked at each other in surprise, "I wonder what he meant by 'a steal of a deal?' Do you think he suspects something?" asked Ramon.

"I don't know but let's get out of here. We're never going to find a car here. There's too many people around." Rodney took Ramon's arm and hurried him toward the car.

It took a while but the scare wore off, "I have another idea," Rodney broke the silence.

"I know where Mom keeps the rent money. Every week she hides some of her salary for rent. By now there should be a hundred at least saved up. We can put it back after we pull the job."

Rodney found only fifty dollars there. He took it and they headed to Bert's Shop to take a look around.

There they were told to try Al's Junk Yard. "I don't have anything here now but I just sent some over to Al's that were on their last legs. You may get a few miles out of one of them."

They found only one worker at the junk yard. He was using a skid loader to move a small pile of rusty metal.

"There's a few that came in in the last few days. I've had no time to strip them down," the rustic old man told them, "And I don't have time to help you right now. The new arrivals are on the front row. So if you want, go see if you can get one of them to crank."

The third one they tried, an old gray Volvo, did crank. They went back in search of the man.

"We found one. How much is it?"

"It's not my car. I just work here." Was the answer, "I don't have time to figure out how much. Take it up with Al," he growled. He had to get down off the noisy skid loader both times he talked with the two. He started to climb back on the machine and to go back to work on the pile of metal.

"But we need it now," Ramon took some crumpled bills out of his pocket and shoved them toward the man. How about I pay fifty dollars now and we can settle with Al later?"

"Fine with me." The man stuffed the bills into the pocket of his black-oil smudged coveralls as he walked off. "I don't know where Al finds these characters," he muttered to himself as he reached for the ring of keys hanging on his belt to lock the gates for the night.

"Who's Al?" Rodney asked as they drove out of the junk yard.

"Damned if I know," Ramon answered, "but we got a car."

Since each one of the three businesses was on opposite ends of the city it took most of the evening to finally find a get-away car.

By this time they were frustrated but determined to carry out their plan.

The liquor store owner had been robbed before and was ready when the two entered. He knew something was up as soon as they walked in. The hoodies they were wearing was a sure give away. When the young thief told him to empty his cash drawer into a bag he complied. He reached for a special bag he kept nearby and opened the special cash drawer and emptied the contents of the drawer into the bag.

Seeing how young the two were, he tried to reason with them, "Now you boys really need to think about what you're doing. I'm not just trying to save my money. I'm thinking about you and where you may be headed in life. You're young men and may have a full life in front of you. But you may not if you continue on a life of crime. Think about what kind of life you'll have in jail."

"*Some thief, he didn't even supply his own the bag,*" he shook his head in disbelief as they headed out the door with fifty ones in a bag which had the store's logo on the front. He called the police to let them know he had been robbed again.

Just as the young thieves sped away in the old junker they heard a loud pop.

"Get down," the driver yelled as he scrunched down himself, "The old geezer's shooting at us."

But it wasn't gunshots they heard. It was the spare tire that had seen its last mile. The last leg had gone. The car swerved out of control, went down an embankment, and landed against a tree.

They first checked to see if the store owner was all right. Then the police, Chief WC Whitt and Deputy Rebecca Stone, went to the accident scene and found the wrecked car as two groggy, bleeding thieves were being loaded into an ambulance. The loot in the bag with the store logo was found in the old gray Volvo.

While the robbers were being booked the officers were laughing about the great heist which netted a total of fifty dollars, an old wrecked car, scratches and bruises, and a night in jail.

"I think a night in our 'hotel' might put a scare into these two. It must be their first attempt," WC commented."

"Yeah and they're not too good at it. I hope this teaches them a lesson. Maybe this will frighten them away from a life of crime," Rebecca answered. She hated to see young people get started on the wrong track. This was the main reason she volunteered at the Teens Life Center.

"Run a tag check to see if the car was stolen."

Rebecca looked up from the computer screen, "The car hasn't been reported as stolen but it isn't registered to either of them. It's registered to a Danny Farmer."

Officer Black of East Side stood in front of the computer his morning cup of coffee in his hand checking on recent activity. This was his normal the routine. Every morning when he first arrived on duty he would check to see what went on in different areas during the night. As he scanned down, everything seemed to be just another night of small time heists.

"Same old, same old," he muttered as he went to get a coffee refill. "Hold on," he told himself as he turned back to the computer, "There was something ..."

He scanned down, "Here it is. Hey Chief would guess what?"

"I don't have time for guessing games. Can't you see I'm busy?" Chief White grinned and turned back to his sausage and egg biscuit.

"Okay, then," Officer Black picked up his morning coffee, walked over to the file cabinet, and pretended to check out a record in the files.

Chief White scooted his chair over to the computer to take a look at what his deputy had been checking on.

The deputy couldn't help but grin, "See anything interesting?"

"All I see is something about a liquor store robbery in the West Side Precinct. It says here the two didn't get away because of a blown tire."

"Yes but their get-away car, a Volvo, is registered to a Danny Farmer."

"Danny Farmer, so?"

"Danny Farmer aka Bobby Dubois at mall the department store."

"Oh, the would-be handbag thief at Sophisticates. The one you remembered being on the prior's list. Looks like you were right to suspect there being more to their story."

"I wonder what the two have in common other than a car."

"I think we should contact west side precinct."

"So the east meets the west."

"Seems like there's more to the petty robbery than we thought," WC commented to Rebecca after he talked with Chief White.

"I guess we need to talk with our two 'smart thieves' we have housed in our 'hotel'," Chief Whitt of the West Side Precinct told Officer Rebecca Stone who was filling out the discharge papers for Ramon and Rodney. I just got a call from east side and something just doesn't feel right to them. It seems we have a match on the owner of the wrecked car.

Rodney and Ramon were brought into separate interrogation rooms and to be questioned again.

Rodney was questioned by Deputy Rebecca Stone, "Now explain to me again how you came to be in possession of the Volvo."

"Okay as I told you before we needed a car so we went to car lots looking for one," Rodney left out the part where they were going to steal one.

"Now let me get this straight. You were already driving a car. Is that right?

"Yes," Rodney gulped.

"Then why did you need another car?"

"You see, it wasn't my car. It was Mom's and she needed it back," Rodney told the little lie and left out an important fact – His mother would kill him if he robbed a store while he was using her car.

"Okay, so where were you going to get this other car?"

"We tried Fred's car lot but we couldn't afford to rent any of them."

"And?" Rebecca prompted.

This line of questioning was getting to Rodney. So he decided to just go through the tedious trail of getting the Volvo.

"Okay, it's a long story. But here goes. We went to several places. Every place we went we were told of another place to go. It was like a scavenger hunt. A man at Fred's Auto told us about Bert's Fix it Shop. We went there. He didn't have any there but he told us that he had sent a few old ones that were not worth fixing to Al's Junk yard to be scrapped. The man there told us we could see if any of them would crank. That's where we found the Volvo."

Ramon was questioned by Chief Whitt, "There's no use telling me you didn't rob the liquor store. We have all the evidence we need to convict you of that. I'm interested in the car you were in. Tell me how you got the Volvo."

"We rented it from somebody named Al."

"What is Al's last name?"

"I don't know. We were told to see someone at Al's Junk Yard."

"Okay, you were riding around in your friend's car. Then you went looking for another one. Somebody told you to go rent one from Al? That doesn't make much sense now does it?"

"First of all it wasn't my friend's car. It was his mother's car."

"Okay you were looking to replace your friend's mother's car. Then what happened?"

Ramon was getting a little angry with of all the questions. He paused as he took control of his temper.

He held up his hand and listed all the places they went by counting on his fingers, "We went a car lot. I went home. We went to a fix-it shop. Then we went to a junk yard. There we found the Volvo. I rented the car from a man there. Does that answer your question?"

"Not quite, why did you go home before you went to the fix-it shop?"

"I uh needed to get money. I forgot and left my billfold at home." He wasn't about to let the Chief know he took the money from his mother's stash. And that he didn't even own a billfold.

After they finished the long story of how they came to have possession of a car that belonged to Danny. A court date was set and they were released.

"Their story was so far-fetched it had to be the truth," laughed Rebecca.

"Yeah," Chief Whitt laughed too as he called Chief White of East Side, "We need to meet to compare notes."

But before the meeting took place another branch of law enforcement decided to join the assembly.

Sheriff Stanley Hayes called West Side city police station, "WC, I was scanning through last night's activities and came across some interesting information. It seems we have a little situation here. I'm not one to be picky but I like to keep things on the up and up so there won't be a problem later on. Did you realize the wreck on Oak Street happened outside the city limits? You know that's in my jurisdiction."

"Now that puts another kink in what started out to be a simple case of robbery," Chief White from East Side wiped his forehead in exasperation and added sarcastically, "I guess we need to include the entire city, county, and anyone else in the surrounding area in on this investigation of the big crime spree we have in our midst."

This simple case of petty larceny turned out to involve two city precincts, the county sheriff, **and Al** –'somebody dared to invade my territory?'

When Rodney and Ramon were released, Al decided to teach the would-be thieves a lesson. He had heard about the two criminals who dared to come into his territory without first contacting him. They were small time crooks but he couldn't let it go. That may encourage others to try it. So he sent a man to put a scare into the 'wonnabe' thieves.

"The man at the junkyard mentioned an Al. Now we know who Al is," Rodney whispered because it hurt too much to talk through his swollen lips.

"Oh so that's Al," Ramon squinted his black eye. "How were we to know we were in his territory? We just needed some money."

CHAPTER 15

KAYLA TIME OFF

Spring break was over and Kayla had returned to the classroom. She still took care of her teaching duties but she could not return to her normal routine. She worried about Sandy and wondered how she was after she had being placed in foster care.

It was a day she was especially worried and needed a break. She asked her teacher's aide to watch the children while they were napping and walked outside to collect her thoughts. The hair on the back of her neck stood on end. She had a feeling someone was watching her every move. This was not the first time. She had felt this before and dismissed it as just her imagination. As she walked around the perimeter of the playground she noticed a movement in the bushes outside the fence. This was not good especially near a school where small children played.

She thought she would be safe since there was a fence between them so she called out, "Whoever you are you need to show yourself. I have dialed the deputy on duty at the school and all I have to do is press send to get him here in a minute's time!"

"It's okay Miss Adair; it's just I Nathanael," he said as he stepped out from behind an azalea in full bloom with his hands out in front of him his palms toward her as if he was warning her off.

"Mr. Harbinger what are you doing out there?" Kayla yelled at him, "Are you stalking me? What do you hope to catch me doing? I'm at school for gosh sake!"

"I assure you I wasn't stalking you. I was just following up on a community interest item when I saw you headed this way. I knew what you would think. So I ducked behind the very bush I was taking a picture of but you saw me anyway. I hid because I didn't want you to think I was spying on you and as you see it didn't work. It made things worse instead. Now you think I'm stalking you."

"Why are you taking pictures of flowers?" Kayla still wasn't convinced.

"This is one of the mundane assignments my boss gave me. I think he's trying to punish me because of the article I printed about you. The county Beautification Club spruced up the grounds by planting these flowering bushes and wanted us at the newspaper to brag about their wonderful contribution to the community."

Kayla could tell he was embarrassed about his assignment, *"Serves him right,"* she agreed with his boss. *"This is nothing like what he put me through."*

"What about the other times? Were you taking pictures of bushes with no blooms?" After she said this she remembered a flash of light one of the times she sensed a presence. "I noticed you have your flash off this time."

"What other times? I assure this is the only time I've been out here and I hope it will be my last."

"He did seem surprised. Should I really believe him? Was he behind the other times that I sensed someone watching me? What was the flash of light? He uses a camera on his job. I can't believe he would forget to shut off the flash. Was he or was it someone else taking pictures of me?"

She looked at her watch, "I have to get back to my class but I think you need to have a talk with the county administrator or someone in charge. These flowers are pretty but they are also a place for predators to hide. Like you just did. The club must not have thought of the potential danger it may put the children in."

As she turned and marched back to the school building she looked back to see if he left. *"No one should be back there. That was the wrong place to demonstrate 'civic duty'!"*

As he walked back to his car Nathanael recollected her words, 'What about the other times? Were you taking pictures of bushes with no blooms?' *"Had there been someone out there watching her? Could she or a child be in danger?"*

Kayla went straight to the office and reported the incident to the principal before she returned to her classroom. The bushes presented a possible danger to the children. She would not have mentioned Nathanael except for the fact if she didn't and someone saw them it would raise questions if she kept it to herself. She had nothing to hide even though she had been falsely accused of kidnapping.

That afternoon the principal called her to his office, "Kayla you have several weeks of vacation you haven't used. I want you to take some time off to settle your nerves."

"What? Is this because I told you the bushes were too close to the school grounds? *His wife must be on the Beautification Club board.*"

"Well no not just that. You seem to be preoccupied. Otherwise why were you out on the playgrounds during school hours?"

"The children were napping and they were being cared for by my aide. I did not leave them alone." She defended her actions.

"I've been fielding questions from concerned parents as well. I think it would be best for us all around if you took some time off." His tone had changed from telling her she needed time off to demanding she do so.

Her mood changed as well. The atmosphere in the office took on a chill. "But I thought you, my fellow teachers, and staff members were backing me and gave witness to my good character. Now I find it was all a sham!"

"You're making this much bigger than it is. But that's beside the point. As I just explained I think it best that you take some time off."

"I would like to know how you **really** feel about me as a teacher and person. Never mind your actions are loud and clear!"

That wasn't the only reason he had given Kayla time off. He needed time to check on an item the records secretary had discovered in Kayla's computer files. The new secretary who was not familiar the school's computer program had misplaced some records. She knew they were in that computer somewhere. She didn't want to appear incompetent. She was sure she could find them on her own. While searching through program folders looking for the lost files she came across Kayla's files. One in particular was interesting.

The principal knew he needed to report this to the law but he wanted to get his facts together first. He didn't want to be charged with falsely accusing one of his teachers. It was a close line he had to walk. He didn't tell Kayla about files found in the school e-mails files. The newly hired secretary had found the file by accident. It looked as if Kayla created an identity file and tried to get Sandy enrolled for next year.

Kayla returned to her room to collect her purse and coat. She tidied the room by picking up the remaining toys and teaching tools the children failed to put back in their proper places. This was her usual routine so she did it without thinking. Her mind was elsewhere. She was angry, hurt, but mostly confused. There must be more to it than a few complaints from a parent.

"Did Nathanael tell her the truth about his reason for being near the school grounds? Was there something else going on? If he wasn't the one spying on her who was? Why did the principal want her to leave? Who were the concerned parents and what were their concerns?"

She organized the boxes and pushed them back on the shelves. She looked around to see if all was in order. Then she took her lesson plan notebook out of the drawer and placed it on her desk. She always kept a detailed lesson plan ready for a substitute in case she had to be out.

"I have been told by substitutes that I leave wonderful easy to follow lesson plans." she remembered with pride. Then her thoughts turned vindictive. She picked up the well-organized notebook and put it in her file cabinet and took out the cold impersonal nondescript curriculum guide for the sub.

"No," she told herself as she thought better of it and changed her mind, *"That would not be fair to the sub, who had nothing to do with my situation. And it certainly wouldn't be fair to the innocent children. And it would not be the Christian thing to do."*

As she placed the lesson plan notebook back on her desk she saw a few personal items she didn't want to leave behind. *"I don't know who will be taking over my duties but I don't want just anybody rummaging through my things."* She sat her purse back down and started collecting them. She had her arms loaded and looked at the stack still left on her desk. There was more she wanted to take, *"This is stupid. I need to stop and think this through,"* she admonished herself as she unloaded her arms and slumped down in a chair.

She was sitting in a child's chair with her arms on her knees and her chin on her fist when Gabe stuck his head in.

"Hey you," Gabe tested the waters.

"Hey yourself," she answered, "Come on in and join the pity party."

He looked around and saw the disarray and carefully chose his words, "Can I help?"

She took down two boxes from the supply shelf and consolidated them. The resulting empty box was used to stow the items she had previously held in her arms.

"Sure take these to my car unless you want your reputation to be tainted by helping me."

It didn't take long. News had already spread throughout the school. She knew her forced leave would again make her appear guilty of something.

Things had begun to cool down somewhat after the first round of suspicions. She had not heard anything from the investigation Erica was doing. So far she had not been charged with anything. Sandy was no longer with her since she was in foster care. But now the Gossip mills were going full swing again.

"Okay," he answered with a grin as he lifted the box, "A little taint never hurt anybody."

The next few days Kayla went on a cleaning spree. She had to take it out on something. It may as well be the house that way her angry energy would not be wasted. Dust rose in a cloud as she tackled the job with a vengeance. Two days later the tiled kitchen floor sparkled. Her spotless refrigerator no longer held leftover food. All her clothes had been color coordinated in the clean closets. But it did little to alleviate the anger and hurt. She couldn't sleep because her mind was still whirling with the unfairness of the whole situation. She was aware her forced 'timeout' made her appear guilty of something.

Kayla not used to having so much time on her hands, didn't know what to do next. And she was antsy to find Sandy's parents. Maybe then she and the whole city could rest easy. But where would she even start in her search? She had exhausted all her resources. Maybe she should hire a private investigator. *"I don't know anything about investigators. Maybe Erica would know one. But the authorities were already on the job."* Did she think she could do better than trained police?

She decided a walk in the park may help sort her thoughts. The YMCA gym was out because she didn't feel like explaining why she was not at school. Even if she wasn't questioned she would be getting 'the look'. The two close friends she could count on were at work so she had no one to talk to. The fast walk was not working so she decided to jog even though she had not done so in years. She was getting out of breath when another jogger came along beside her.

She stopped running and bent down with her hands on her knees and wheezed, "Why," puff, "are you," puff, wheeze, "follow ing me?" she asked Nathanael.

"Why don't you sit down and rest long enough to catch your breath?" he suggested as he placed his hand on the small of her back and maneuvered her over to the park bench.

"I wasn't following you, well not until I saw you in the park. But I do want to talk with you. Since it's close to noon, why don't we stop by the restaurant for lunch? There's one on the right just as we leave the park."

"Is it that late? No wonder I'm out of breath. I've been here since nine. Why not take him up on the offer? Hashing it out with 'Mr. Muckraker' would be better than fuming alone at home."

"Okay it's a date. No, no, it's not a date. I mean I'll meet you there."

"How pathetic is this? I'm getting so pitiful I'm willing to cavort with the enemy. But I need to vent my anger. It may as well be toward one of my tormentors."

Nathanael had heard through the grapevine she had been sent home after the incident at the playground. He called Talitha when he heard about her dismissal to make sure it was true. He opened his mouth to apologize for her plight. But he decided it would appear he was still trying to get another news item.

Instead he tried to explain his reasoning about the article in the newspaper. "When I saw you being hauled off by EMS and DSS taking a screaming child from your house I assumed the worse. I didn't know you so I acted on my assumptions. And what's even worst I printed it. I didn't know I was going to cause you so much trouble. I now see how much my actions have damaged your reputation. Sometimes I just don't think. I just act."

"You think so? People whisper behind my back or DSS takes a screaming child from my home while I'm wheeled out on a stretcher headed for the psych ward? Against my wishes I might add. So you think you may have caused a little trouble for me?" The sarcastic smile on her face didn't hide the angry fire in her eyes.

"You have every right to be mad…."

"Mad what makes you think I'm mad? Just because the things I just mentioned are sandwiched in between two horrible pictures you splashed on the daily news and your stunt on the playground causing me to be jobless. Why would I be mad?"

Over the next few days Nathanael sought Kayla out. She needed to vent her frustrations. He secretly volunteered to be her punching bag. He thought he owed her that much. Each time they talked it became easier for her to accept his apologies. They began to accept each other's side of the situation. Kayla could understand Nathanael's job was to gather news. Maybe she was being too hard on him. But he had clearly overstepped this privilege by reporting an item about her that was incorrect. Nathanael began to feel he had without a doubt abused his role as news reporter. But there was still that nibbling in the back of his reporter mind. Who was Sandy and why did she come to Kayla? He found Kayla to be a compassionate woman especially when it came to underprivileged children. She seemed to be drawn to children. When they walked in the park she would stop to watch their antics. There had to be more to the story. But was this just his imagination? Was he seeing more than was there? She wasn't the only one smiling at the cute children. A lot of people especially women took note of the children as they played. Even he noticed how happy they were as they scampered around. Besides she was a teacher of small children. Why wouldn't she notice them?

"Nathanael you're early," Kayla said as she opened the door. "Oh, it's you Gabe," She was surprised to see Gabe standing at the door with a small basket.

"Someone sent this to school for you. The secretary didn't know what to do with it. She didn't want to tell the woman who delivered it you were on leave."

"Won't you come in?" Kayla held the door open for him. "I'm sorry I thought…

"No, no," he interrupted her. "I'm… uh… you're expecting company. I was on my way home from school and thought I'd drop it off," Gabe pushed the basket into her hands then backed away and rushed down the steps.

"She thought I was Nathanael. No wonder she didn't meet me for our usual Friday night outing," Gabe felt a pang of jealousy as he fled toward his car.

Kayla saw the hurt in Gabe's eyes. She had not seen him in a week. The first time she didn't meet Gabe for their usual get together was the evening she met Sandy. Surely Gabe understood that. But last Friday was her fault. She had not realized what day it was until it was too late. She wanted to explain this to Gabe but he had left in a hurry and didn't give her a chance.

She and Nathanael had been curled up on her sofa watching a romantic movie. As the movie continued they tended to get more comfortable. Nathan's arm which had started out on the back of the sofa ended draped around Kayla and her head rested his shoulder. By the time the movie ended they were wrapped in each other's arms. In the spirit of the moment he reached over and gave her a tender kiss. It seemed so natural her arms went around his neck as she returned the kiss. When the tender kiss turned into passion it surprised both of them.

They were laughing about it when Nathanael grinned and teased, "Well I guess Friday the thirteenth isn't a bad day after all."

"Friday?" she gasped as she jumped up. She felt so chagrined. *"Gabe, how could I be so thoughtless? He must be wondering what happened to me when I didn't show up."* She grabbed Nathanael by the arm, "You have to leave," she told him as she shoved him toward the door.

"What did I say that was wrong?" Nathanael was puzzled by her reaction. "You don't seem to be that type of person to be superstitious."

"It has nothing to do with what you did or said but you have to leave now," she said as she ushered him out the door.

She had lived her life on schedule until she met Sandy. Then everything began to get out of kilter. She couldn't even keep up with days. She didn't realize it was Sunday and failed to show up at church. She didn't meet Gabe on Friday. Evidently she was shirking her responsibility at school because she was forced to take time off. Now she had time on her hands and didn't know what to do. The evenings especially were difficult. She usually spent her time grading papers and planning the next day's activities. Now that it was no longer necessary she worried about Sandy. There was nothing she could do. But it still kept her awake. That was the reason she had spent so much time with Nathanael. He was filling the empty space. Or was she kidding herself? She was beginning to enjoy the time she spent with him. She even found their arguments invigorating. Now the kiss made things complicated.

She looked at the odd basket in her hands. Gabe had handed it to her and left quickly as if he was trying to escape. It had only an apple in it. There was no logo on the basket to indicate the florist. There was no card from the sender.

"What did Gabe say 'Someone brought it to school.'? He didn't mention who sent it."

"Talitha thank goodness you're here," Kayla stepped into the travel agency and looked around the room. Travel brochures were scattered over several tables. Two couples looked up as she walked in. They were thumbing through booklets waiting their turn. Talitha was shaking hands with a client who was leaving.

"I need to talk with you. But it looks like you're very busy. I'll see you later."

Talitha saw the look on Kayla's face and caught her arm as she turned to leave, "I'm never too busy to help a friend and you look like you need help."

Talitha turned to the two waiting couples, "Miss Smolt and Mr. Wilt will be with you shortly. I'm sure they will take good care of you."

"An emergency just came up and I need to leave," she told the secretary, "I'll let you lock up."

"I hate to take you away from your clients," Kayla apologized.

"Don't worry about it. They're walk-ins. This happens often especially at closing time. But they're welcome. We give them a short version, some brochures to browse, and schedule an appointment if they want to plan a trip. Now what's this worried look about?"

"Gabe dropped off this odd basket that was delivered to my school. I thought he was Nathanael when the doorbell rang. I think I hurt his feelings when I called him Nathanael. I don't know who sent the basket. There is no note no tag from a florist. I sent Nathanael away right in the middle of a movie we were watching. I tried calling Gabe but he doesn't answer."

"Kayla you're rambling." Talitha placed her hand on her Kayla's arm. They were sitting at a table in the corner of Tim's Diner. "Take a breath to settle your nerves. We have all evening. Heck we have all night if that's what it takes."

Kayla took a sip of her coffee and sighed, "It may take a week."

"Now that you brought up the subject haven't you been seeing a lot of Mr. Harbinger lately? I thought he was the enemy."

"Well he was there. You and Gabe were working."

"I think there's more to it than that."

"He's just someone to talk to," she dismissed her comment.

"I'm not about to tell her he kissed me while we watched the movie."

"Doesn't he have a job as well?"

"You're right, now that you mention it; he should have been working too."

"Maybe he **was** working and you just didn't recognize it. Now let's go see that basket. What's so odd about it?"

"It has just one apple. No note. No florist logo. Just a basket with one apple. Do you think it's odd as well? Or is it just me being paranoid?"

A piece of paper fell out of Gabe's car and he stepped on it as he got out. He reached down to retrieve it and made a dash to the door to avoid getting too wet as he entered the grocery. As he pushed the cart he opened the soggy envelope, "What an odd note. It makes no sense at all. Why was it in my car?"

He was checking out at the register when his cell phone rang. 'Kayla' was on the screen. Since it was still raining he rushed to put the groceries in the trunk. "I'll call her later."

He returned her call as he put away his purchases, "I'm sorry I didn't answer the phone when you called. I was busy at the checkout counter."

"Thanks for calling me back. I wanted to ask you about that basket you brought to me. You said it was from school. There was no note with it. Do you know who sent it?"

"No, I don't. But I thought there was a card but I didn't look at it."

Then it dawned on him, "Wait, a card fell out of my car. The ink was smudged on the envelope because it fell into a puddle of water and

I stepped on it. I don't know if it was from the basket or not. I opened it to see what it was. It had the strangest message, like it was in code. Some alphabet letters and a number, one hundred I think, with several k's. You're not connected to the Klan are you?" he asked with a nervous laugh.

Kayla hesitated then asked, "Could you bring it over? I'd like to see it."

"I uh must have dropped it in the store." Gabe said as he searched through the bags. "I'll go back and see if I can find it."

"Don't worry about it. It's probably a practical joke. There seems to be a lot of that going on since my pictures appeared in the news."

"That was Gabe answering my call. There was a note with the basket but apparently he lost it. He said it fell out of his car into a puddle and he stepped on it."

Talitha and Kayla sat staring at the basket after Gabe called.

"What?" Talitha asked as Kayla looked at her with questioning eyes.

"He also asked about my connections to the Klan." Kayla shrugged her shoulders as she waved her teacup in the air. "I wonder what that was about?"

They were still puzzling over the basket and Klan connections when the doorbell rang.

He was hesitant to go to Kayla's because of her reaction the last time he was there. "*I hope this isn't another awkward moment. She was expecting Nathanael when I showed up. But she did ask me to bring the note over. I should have called first though. She won't be expecting me. She doesn't know I found it. I hope this doesn't get too awkward like the last time.*" His pride was still smarting as he remembered the time she mistook him for Nathanael. As he turned to go back down the front steps the door opened.

"Gabe, my goodness you're soaked. Get in here and dry off," Kayla reached out and tugged him inside. "Take that wet coat off and let me get a towel for your hair."

"I found it," he turned and held up a plastic bag to explain his presence. Then he saw Talitha, "Oh I didn't know you had company."

"*Thank goodness it isn't Nathanael.*"

"It's okay. I'm so glad you came. Talitha and I were discussing this basket you delivered. Why would anyone send just one apple? And your comment about the Klan, what on earth was that about?"

"You'll see when you look at the note. It was stuck to the bottom of the grocery bag," he explained where he found it.

He handled it carefully as he took the wet note out of a quart size plastic bag. It was wrapped in the paper towel he had used in an attempt to blot it dry. He placed it on the table and peeled back the towel to reveal the words, 'C UR E-files' 100(KKKKK)'. "Do you know what that means?"

Both Gabe and Talitha watched as Kayla sank down in a chair with a heavy sigh. They didn't know what to think. This wasn't like Kayla.

"Maybe Gabe has forgiven me for my faux pas. There were two now that I think about it. I missed our regular Friday night outing and mistakenly thought he was Nathanael at the door. He was so shocked when I called him Nathanael. He seems a little uncomfortable. But what is the old saying? 'What are best friends for?' And these are my two best friends."

"Wait here," she said as she braced her hands on the chair arms to help her stand and slowly walked to her office to get the other notes. One was a copy of the one she gave to the police. She put the other two beside the third.

There lay all three:

1. *I saw you kidnap the child which by the way is a federal offence. $500,000 in used bills will keep me quiet and **you out of federal prison**. You have one week. I'll send details later.*
2. *2nd time = jail for sure*
3. *C UR E-files' 100(KKKKK)*

"Did you show these to the police?" Talitha asked with a worried look.

"They have the first one but I was afraid to show them the second one."

"What were you afraid of?" asked Gabe as he reread the second one, "2nd time equals jail for sure. What does it mean anyway?"

"After I got over the shock from the first note, I thought it might be a sick joke. Now that I've received three notes I don't think that anymore," Kayla answered. "Someone must have found out what happened when I was a teen. That was the first time I was accused of kidnapping. So this would be the second time. That's why I was afraid to show the notes to the police. I thought the files were closed but apparently someone found them anyway."

"I know something must have happened to make your childhood a sensitive subject. But when you told me you didn't like to talk about it, I respected your feelings. That's why I didn't ask again. But now I think is the time. We're friends. Gabe and I know you. It couldn't be that bad. What happened?" Talitha asked.

"I grew up in an orphanage. I don't like to talk about it because people tend to feel sorry for orphans." She paused as if to end the conversation.

"What happened? Why were you accused of kidnapping?" Talitha asked again.

She decided it was time to share with her two close friends. "The orphanage wasn't too bad until I became a teenager. That's when I thought I was smarter than the adults. Tina, one of the children came to the orphanage just after she was born. She wasn't placed in as foster home because she had a club foot. She was passed over by couples wanting a perfect child to adopt. Even though the doctor assured them the deformity was minor and could be corrected no one wanted to take the chance. Tina was placed in braces to correct the twisted foot. But it seemed to me the nursery workers didn't want to spend the extra time it took to care for this 'damaged child'. So at the age of twelve I was allowed to be her caretaker. By the time she was three I had practically raised her myself. Even though she was able to walk like normal children she still had the stigma of being a cripple. She was bullied by the other children. The house mother just ignored it and did nothing to stop it. It seemed to me she was being mistreated. That's when I took matters into my own hands. At the age of fifteen I ran away from the orphanage and took Tina with me. I was going to find a job. The two of us would be a family. Unfortunately we were found by the police and returned to the orphanage. The case was handled by DSS and closed because I was underage. That is I thought it was closed. Things didn't go well after that. My punishment was harsh. I was given the most unpleasant duties. I won't go into details. I don't want to relive them and you don't want to hear them. I was mistrusted and watched closely. I was not allowed to see Tina. That was the most heartbreaking thing of all. It was like taking a child away from her mother. I was told by one of the girls that Tina cried herself to sleep for several weeks after that. So as you can see I didn't want to bring attention to the notes which referred to kidnaping in my past. But somehow someone found those records and is using them to extort money from me."

Kayla swallowed and held back tears that threatened to surface, "I'm not worried about myself so much. But I've seen how children can be manipulated. I shudder to think what Sandy, this innocent child, has gone through to make her think I am her mother."

Gabe and Talitha wrapped their arms around Kayla. They were quiet for several minutes. What could they say? They were two good friends sharing a moment of support for Kayla.

The three of them glared at the third note willing it to give up its secret.

"Now this last one 'C UR E-files' 100(KKKKK)'; it was delivered to the school. Why? That must mean something but what?" Gabe wondered aloud.

"It must have something to do with school," Talitha added.

"I don't think 'kkkkk' has anything to do with the Klan,"

Kayla thought for a while. "Look! It's mathematical; one hundred times five k. Five hundred thousand that's the amount they are demanding. And e-files! There must be something in my e-files at school."

Kayla rushed to her office and logged on her computer. Kayla was surprised when she opened her files. There was an enrollment form filled out for a Sandy Adair listing Kayla as the mother.

"What? I didn't do this! Someone has placed this in my files," Kayla pushed away from her computer in frustration and started pacing.

"Why would anyone do that? Have you had a problem with anyone at school?" Talitha asked as she followed her around the house.

"I haven't had any serious problems until now that is. Oh we've had our differences like most places of employment but nothing serious. We don't always agree on everything. I can't think of a thing that would cause someone to do this to me."

"I thought our files at school were secure. If someone could hack into your files to do this there's no telling what else they could do with the school's files," Gabe began to worry about their confidential records.

"I thought our files were safe too. Who could do this? Only school personal has access. That must be the reason for my forced vacation. Monday morning I'm going straight to school to find out what's really going on."

Erica couldn't help but wonder why anyone would pick Kayla. She seemed to be such an unlikely candidate to extort. But it was Erica's nature to follow up on her intuitions. There had to be more to the story. That was why she spent her spare hours on line searching for anything connected to Kayla. She found nothing of significance in her background check. The search led her to the orphanage where Kayla grew up. She left the home at the age of eighteen. Using money set aside in a college fund she got her teaching degree. Then she was hired to teach. That was it. The trail was cold. There had to be more. There was one puzzling thing, the college fund. Who set that up? Was that the 'more' that was nibbling at her brain?

But Erica wasn't the only one working on the internet searching through Kayla's background. Lilly White was determined to find something about her. She started with the present and worked her way backward. Even if he was working on the story, Nathanael was spending too much time with Kayla. He no longer stopped by her desk to talk. She had been there for him. She had watched his back and fielded his mistakes. If she could find something she may get back in his good graces. However the search ended the same as with Erica. Kayla had spent her youth in an orphanage. Then she attended college and got a teaching job. She had tried every avenue. It was the end of a boring story. Her last resource was the archives of the newspaper. It was two AM and Lilly was ready to shut her computer off when a match popped up. She had found a hit. It was such a short item she nearly missed it. It was a missing person alert. A three-year old child and a teenager were missing from an orphanage. The article stated the child may be with the teen, Kayla Adair. Anyone having any information about the two was asked to contact the police or orphanage. Lilly was ecstatic. This was a gold nugget. A small one she admitted but it should get Nathanael's attention. She couldn't wait to tell him. He may have been right after all. I wonder if that's the reason she's a teacher; so she could be close to children.

CHAPTER 16

KAYLA SHOWS LETTERS TO POLICE

The letter with instructions came Monday morning before Kayla could get to the school as she had planned. At four AM Kayla was to put the money in Ollie's Convenient Store's trash bin in a Happy Pet dog food bag.

"That does it. I'm going straight to the police station and demand an explanation. They have to know something about what is going on. Otherwise why am I constantly being questioned and followed? Maybe Nathanael has something to do with it. Maybe he has been stringing me along pretending to be interested. He even kissed me. Just how far will he go to get a story? What was he really doing back there at my school just before I was asked to take a leave of absence? Who could be behind the extortion letters? Is it someone at school? How else could they get access to my records?"

Kayla was trying to decide what to do as she dressed for the day. As she drove toward the police station she passed the Daily News building. On an impulse she made a U-turn and entered the building.

Lilly was surprised and caught off guard when Kayla entered with a determined look on her face. She was the last person she wanted to see at this moment. She tried not to show the guilt she felt. She had spent the night looking into Kayla's background and found out about her taking a child from the orphanage. She had not yet had the chance to tell Nathanael her news.

"Kayla uh I mean Miss Adair," she stuttered. "What can I do for you?"

"I'd like to see Mr. Harbinger."

"He isn't here right now. I don't know when he will be in. Is there something I can do?"

"No. Just tell him I stopped by." She really didn't know what she was going to say but she needed to know what he knew about her situation. Since he seemed to keep track of her whereabouts she wanted to know what else he knew about her. Then she thought about how he showed up at the oddest times and places. It didn't dawn on her before. Now it was unsettling.

She turned to leave as Nathanael walked in the door.

"Kayla," he smiled as he took her hand, "What a nice surprise. Have you had breakfast?"

"No," she answered. All her questions disappeared as she looked into the deep blue eyes and remembered the passionate kiss.

"Good. Neither have I," he took her elbow and was ushering her out the door when Lilly stopped him.

"Nat ... Sir you have an important message," Lilly rushed over and handed him a hastily written note.

They were sitting in a booth side by side waiting for their order when Nathanael took Lilly's note out of his pocket. Kayla saw the word kidnapper before he hastily put it back in his pocket.

Kayla quickly recovered from the shock and forced a sweet smile, "What was that a hot tip on a news item?"

"It's nothing important, just something I need to follow up on," he shrugged.

But he wondered about the note, *"What did Lilly mean 'She is a kidnapper'?"*

"So it seems the note is about something he doesn't want to discuss. Is he hiding something about me? Why was Lilly in a rush to see that he got her note?"

The word kidnapper on the note made Kayla forget about his blue eyes. It made her more of a mind to get answers. Was he still after her for a story? Is that why he's been so friendly lately? She was about to confront him when the ping of a text sounded on her phone.

"Where are you? I thought you were coming to school today," was the text from Gabe.

"I'm sorry Nathanael. I have to answer this," Kayla excused herself and left the restaurant.

"Something came up. I'll tell you about it later," she texted back.

Lilly's note changed her mind about breakfast and Nathanael. *"I'll have to question Mr. Harbinger later,"* she decided. *"I need to get to the police station."*

The last note from the extortionist was the final straw. And the note Lilly slipped Nathanael made her more determined. She needed the authorities on her side not against her. She made a phone call to Gabe's lawyer friend, Wyle Morgan. It wouldn't hurt to get professional advice first.

"Come on by my office," he instructed her. "I can shuffle my schedule around to see you." He wanted to meet her face to face. He could tell a lot about a client when he looked them in the eye.

She told him everything she could think of that could be connected to Sandy and the notes, including her stay at the orphanage.

"I see no need for me to come with you at this time. I think it would better for you if you go in voluntarily. However, if at any time during the interview you feel uncomfortable about a question feel free to stop the inquisition and call me.

Chief White was in the conference room with his main investigators. It was time for each team to give updates. It was frustrating. There were no new leads on the O'Malley Construction Company murder-robbery case.

A deputy stuck his head in and announced, "Chief a Miss Adair is here to see you."

"Thank goodness I hope she can shed light on one case at least. Erica you and Mike stay. The rest of you get out there and find something. The O'Malley case is getting cold."

"Mike, bring me up to date on the kidnapping case. I need to know the latest before I talk with Miss Adair," the chief asked as they walked toward the smaller interrogation room.

Mike's stammering indicated he knew very little about the case.

"Erica I need you to stay. Mike, take Billy's place on traffic detail. He asked for some time off. Tell him he's free to go visit his parents," the chief excused him with a frown.

"Traffic duty! That's worse than the silly kidnapping case. I bet if I was on the O'Malley case I could find out what happened." Mike mumbled as he headed out to relieve Billy.

"Okay Erica, you bring me up to date before I bring in Miss Adair." Chief White asked as he positioned the chairs to his advantage.

Erica's reports were always factual and to the point. "There's nothing much new. She was put on leave from school after she had a run in with Mr. Harbinger on the school grounds. I inquired about the reason and was told it was a personnel decision and therefore confidential. Since then they have been seen together. I assume they are on friendly terms now. When I researched her background I found she grew up in an orphanage but I didn't found anything out of the ordinary. That's about it."

"You have the first note," Kayla said as she placed the other notes on the table for Chief White and Erica to see. "I know you are busy so I'll try to be brief."

She gave her version of what each one meant. "The first one arrived after I met Sandy at the mall and took her home with me. It accused me of kidnapping. It shocked me at first. Then I thought it was a joke. That's when my syrupy picture was pasted on the front page of the Daily News. The next one seems to be alluding to an incident which happened when I was fifteen. I was living in an orphanage and left with a child who I thought was being mistreated. I didn't show you the second note because it seemed to be connected to my stay in the orphanage. I left with a child I thought needed my protection. I was afraid you would think I kidnapped children. I'm not worried about myself anymore. I'm worried about Sandy."

"The third one was harder to decipher. I found someone had hacked into my computer files and placed an enrollment request there." She placed a copy of the request beside the note.

"This last one came this morning." She pointed to the one instructing her to leave money behind a convenience store. "I don't know what to do about all this."

"Thank you for coming in Miss Adair. I put Officer Key in charge of investigating your case and she has done an excellent job so far. I assure you we are all concerned about Sandy as well. Erica will be in touch if we need more information from you. Be sure to keep us posted if anything else comes up."

Kayla left with a heavy heart in spite of the assurances Chief White gave her. She still felt there was something that could be done.

After Kayla left Chief White turned to Erica. "This case is more serious than I first thought. You may need to get a full report from Miss Adair later but right now I'm going to assign two other officers to work with you on the case. I want you to bring them up to date."

Erica gave the two officers a copy of her investigative reports and Kayla's extortion notes. "Miss Adair is more concerned about Sandy than she is about any threat to her. I have tried to find out how Sandy is doing but Mrs. Latimore at child protection services refuses to release any information."

Erica's cell phone rang the ID showed 'Latimore CPS'.

"What a coincidence," Erica said as she answered the call.

"Hello Mrs. Latimore I hope you have good news about Sandy." Erica called her name for the benefit of the other officers in the room.

"Miss Key I hope you don't mind my calling you. Your number was in my log from when you called to ask for the interview."

"I don't mind at all, Mrs. Latimore. How can I help you?"

"I called to see if you have anything new about Sandy. Have you found her family yet?"

"You want us to tell you what we know but you refuse to tell us anything about her."

"I'm at the station and my colleagues and I were just discussing the case when you called. Do you mind if I put you on speaker?"

Mrs. Latimore thought for a moment and decided, "That would be fine."

"We have no news. Can you tell us how Sandy is doing?"

"Actually she isn't doing well. I'm worried about her. I know this may be unorthodox but I feel that in the best interest of the child we get family court involved as soon as possible."

From the mummers in the room it seemed they agreed. They also agreed that it would be almost impossible to follow proper legal procedures. No one had been formally accused of a crime. There wasn't enough evidence to accuse Kayla of kidnapping. She just took the child home with her. They couldn't find a family member to charge with child neglect.

Mrs. Latimore contacted family court and explained the situation. Because it was a pressing matter a hearing was set for the next day. Since the case involved a child and was so unusual the judge decided on an informal hearing. And she wanted to hear from all those involved.

Family court was more concerned with the child's welfare but Kayla was so closely connected it would be difficult to separate the two. If in the course of the hearing there was sufficient evidence found to charge Kayla with a crime the case would be turned over to another court.

Chapter 17

CHILD CUSTODY

"Record the child's name as Sandy," Judge Lawson instructed the recorder. "I don't want these proceedings to continue to call her 'the child in question'.

Miss Sumner manager of Sophisticates gave her account of what happened, "Miss Adair brought Sandy to one of my clerks who sent her to my office. Miss Adair asked me if anyone had reported a missing child. I checked with my employees and made an announced over the loud speaker. No one in my shop was looking for Sandy. Deputy Black who was filling in as security for my shop was busy with a shop lifter, so I called Mrs. Brown who was in charge of mall security, to tell her a child had been found. All the while Sandy kept calling Miss Adair 'Mommy'. We, Miss Adair, Mrs. Brown, and I searched for Sandy's parent. No one came to claim her."

Mrs. Brown took up the tale where Miss Sumner left off, "There were several others involved in the search. We checked the surveillance tapes and found nothing. By that time it was getting very late. I did run a quick background check on Miss Adair and found no red flags. Sandy was reluctant to let anyone but Miss Adair near her. So we let Kayla take Sandy home with her."

After that the subject changed to the incident at Kayla's house, Deputies Key and Core of the police department, a paramedic from EMS, Mrs. Brown who called 911, and Talitha, Kayla's friend were questioned.

"Mr. Harbinger you were asked to appear, even though I have my suspicions that you would be here anyway. Since you caused a near riot with your report that Sandy had been kidnapped, I want to hear why you decided Sandy was kidnapped."

"I followed the emergency vehicle and police to her home. I saw a social worker take a child from the home. I learned Miss Adair did not have a child. Even though Sandy insisted Miss Adair was her mother, her fellow teachers and acquaintances said Miss Adair did not have a child. Miss Adair herself said she didn't have a child. The security guard told me Miss Adair said she was not the child's mother. Yet she was seen leaving the mall with a child. Later she went shopping for clothes for Sandy and she let Sandy pick out food she liked at a grocery, and she was also spotted trying to hide a child under her coat."

Mrs. Latimore of Child Protection Services was questioned next. "The foster parent is concerned. Sandy isn't eating much and doesn't sleep because of nightmares. It isn't unusual for a foster child to be withdrawn but it is unusual for one so young. She just sits alone and doesn't play."

Mrs. Latimore explained how and why she took the child from Kayla's home. "We went to visit Miss Adair to check on Sandy after Mrs. Brown called and reported a child had been found. She explained the situation including the fact that Miss Adair had taken Sandy to her home. When we rang Miss Adair's doorbell she shut the door in our face. Then we heard a child scream. We entered the house and found Miss Adair holding Sandy down on the floor. By her own statement at the mall, she was not the mother. Yet she took the child home with her. She took her shopping for clothes a clear indication she intended to keep her. Several people saw her shopping with the child. It was reported to us that she tried to hide her under her coat when she went shopping."

Character witnesses especially fellow teachers, Talitha, and Gabe went to Kayla's defense when they were allowed to speak.

Then Kayla was asked to give her account of what happened at the mall as well as the emergency at her house. Judge Lawson dismissed the reports of Kayla's suspicious behavior because Kayla had already stated she was not Sandy's mother. And she dispelled the accusation of hiding Sandy under her coat. It was raining and Sandy didn't have a rain coat so she was shielding her from the rain.

"Is there any additional information I need to hear?" Judge Lawson asked Mrs. Latimore.

"Yes I would like to present Dr. Powell."

"I'll speak with the doctor in my chambers," was her answer as she rose from her chair and nodded.

"Okay Dr. Powell let's hear what you have to say."

"Physically Sandy was in good health when I first saw her. But she seems to have an unusual fear of doctors. As soon as Sandy saw me she wrapped her arms around herself and started crying and begged for Mommy. By the time I finished the physical examination she was shivering so she was near to the point of hysteria. When I saw her a week later she was a different person. She had lost weight and was subdued. Her foster parent was concerned about her health and brought her back."

The judge opened the chamber door, excused doctor, and called to the bailiff, "Would you ask Mrs. Latimore to step in here please?"

"Mrs. Latimore I want to see the child," a recess was called and Mrs. Latimore was instructed to bring Sandy to her chambers after lunch.

Nathanael had positioned himself in an inconspicuous place in the corridor and saw Sandy as she was led into the judge's chamber. She was not the same feisty child that he had witnessed when she was taken from Kayla's home. She slid her feet as she was pulled along by Mrs. Latimore. It was obvious the child was miserable and terrified. His heart went out to her when he heard her whimper as she was led into the judge's chambers. The heavy door closed behind her. He could only imagine what the poor child felt. The sound was like a metal door to a dungeon being closed shutting her in. The small child was surrounded by strangers; two giant adults loomed over her.

"Now I know how Kayla must have felt when the child shied away from the other adults at the mall. Kayla was the only one she trusted and she trusted her with her heart and soul. To Sandy Kayla was her Mommy. How could she not take her home with her?" Nathanael's opinion of Kayla just made a ninety degree turn. *"No way would I have left that defenseless little child there to fend for herself against those she so obviously feared."*

The judge saw how frightened Sandy was of both her and Mrs. Latimore. "From the accounts I have heard so far, it seems the only person Sandy isn't afraid of is Kayla Adair who Sandy claims is her mother. This child will not be comfortable with my questioning her. I have no other option. I have to ask Kayla to join us."

As soon as the door opened Sandy saw Kayla, "Mommy, Mommy," she cried as she ran out to Kayla with her arms reaching out to her. Kayla ran to Sandy and leaned over to scoop her up in her arms. Sandy leaped at Kayla and they both landed on the floor. They sat on the floor as they squeezed each other. A tear slid down Kayla's cheek as she placed her hands around the child's face and saw dark circles around the sunken tear filled eyes.

Talitha and Gabe came rushing over to check on Kayla and Sandy. Nathanael started to rush over when Kayla and Sandy landed on the floor. But Talitha and Gabe reached them first.

"Hey Miss Talitha," Sandy smiled as she wiped her face with the back of her hand and looked up at her, "Who is he?" she was apprehensive as Gabe reached his hand out to help Kayla up.

"*I don't know what to think about Kayla. It's a quandary. In the beginning I was just after a story. She was some whacko woman who tried to take a child at the mall. She was in a snit when she accosted me at my office. But since I have gotten to know her personally I find she's a likeable person. I've enjoyed her company. Maybe I was wrong about her.*" Nathanael admitted to himself as he put away his camera. "*Old habits are hard to break. But Lilly's note is troublesome.*"

"Why don't we go to my office?" Judge Lawson gestured toward the doorway.

Kayla took Sandy's hand and led her inside.

"I don't like it in there," Sandy whispered to Kayla as she reluctantly went in the judge's chamber.

"Who are these people?" she quietly asked Kayla as she looked at Judge Lawson and Mrs. Latimore.

"This is Judge Lawson. Say hello to Judge Lawson," Kayla instructed.

"Hello Judge Lawson," Sandy complied.

"Now say hello to Mrs. Latimore."

Sandy looked up at Kayla, "I don't like Mrs. Latimore."

"That's okay. You don't have to say 'hello' but you can be respectable and say 'Mrs. Latimore'."

Sandy pressed close to Kayla's legs as she looked at Mrs. Latimore and repeated, "Mrs. Latimore."

"And this is Mr. Gabe a good friend of mine."

"Hello Mr. Gabe," she smiled at him as if to say 'a friend of Mommy is a friend of mine'.

Judge Lawson was impressed by the exchange between Kayla and Sandy. She was also impressed with the intellect Sandy seemed to have. "I did tell Sandy who I was but I guess she was too upset to hear," she explained to Kayla.

Then she crouched down and asked Sandy, "Since you don't like my office, would you like to see the courtroom instead?"

"Yes please. Will you wear a black robe too?" she asked.

That took Judge Lawson by surprise, "*She must have been in a courtroom before or she watched a Judge program on TV.*"

"I certainty will," she replied as she turned back toward her chambers to get the robe.

"All rise," instructed the bailiff in a booming voice. Judge Lawson entered from a side room and sat behind the bench. For Sandy's benefit this was going to be a semiformal hearing after all.

She sat on several cushions in the witness chair and swung her feet as she answered Judge Lawson's questions. The only information the judge got out of her was her name which was Sandy Adair and she lived with Mommy and Mommy's name was Kayla. Judge Lawson was fascinated by the difference in Sandy's demeanor when she was with Kayla. She changed from a frightened withdrawn child to a happy precocious toddler.

Judge Lawson told Sandy she could return to sit beside Kayla and addressed some of the people in the courtroom. "Mrs. Brown in your deposition you stated that you did a background check on Miss Adair and found nothing. Is this correct?"

"Yes that is correct Your Honor," was the answer.

"And Mrs. Latimore you found nothing when you checked?"

"Yes Your Honor.

"Miss Adair since you have already kept Sandy at your home, I take it you would be willing to take her again?"

"I would be happy to Your Honor. That is until her parents are located."

Judge Lawson instructed Mrs. Latimore to provide the proper paperwork to grant temporary custody of Sandy to Kayla Adair. "Since we don't know Sandy's legal name, list her name as Sandy Doe. I hope I don't have to remind both of you to keep in touch with each other to make sure Sandy's best interest is at heart. Is that understood?"

"No, Your Honor. I mean yes Your Honor," Mrs. Latimore was flustered as to how to answer the judge's two comments.

"We understand, Your Honor, and we will keep in touch with each other to make Sandy's welfare top priority."

Judge Lawson made sure Sandy was looking before she pounded the gavel for Sandy's benefit and announced, "Court is dismissed".

Talitha and Gabe joined Kayla and Sandy as they rose to leave.

"Time to celebrate," Gabe smiled as he took Sandy's hand, "How would you like a large chocolate milk shake?"

"With a cherry on top?" Sandy asked as she smiled up at Gabe.

"Of course with a cherry on top, is there any other kind?"

Chapter 18

WHY GOD?

Even though Kayla was happy to take Sandy home with her, she wanted the child to be reunited with her family. She was confused as to why God had placed her in her hands. It had to be God's doing. There didn't seem to be any other explanation. Why else were the two of them, such an unlikely pair, thrown together?

"If I am to comply with the DSS rules I need to fix up a bedroom for Sandy. But that will make it seem a more permanent arrangement and set me up for heartbreak later on when I have to give her up," Kayla thought as she looked at Sandy who was sound asleep on her bed. She was now content. It was as if she was home where she should be.

It had been a long eventful day for them both. The court had granted Kayla temporary custody because Sandy was not faring well at the foster home where she had been placed. Talitha and Gabe had long since gone home after seeing them home. Now Kayla was left to her wonderings. So much had happened in such a short time. Her life had been turned upside down. Her serene lifestyle had become a hive of activity. Some of which was not pleasant. Her life was now an open book thanks a reporter's overactive imagination. For someone who cherished her privacy this was quite upsetting. She was also now out of work. Even if it may be a short repast she felt as if she had been fired. This too was a first for her. As she sat pondering the whole situation she started to talk it over with God.

"Why did you choose **me** to take care of Sandy? Why was Sandy placed in this precarious position? Is she in some kind of danger that I need to protect her? If so why **I** was chosen for this task? What is Your plan,

Lord? What do you want me to do? Do you want me to find her parents? Give me some kind of hint. Give me the wisdom to follow Your direction.

She sat mulling over the situation. "I don't know how long she'll be with me. She doesn't seem to be missing her family. She insists I am her mother. If she doesn't give us some hint as to her family, how I am going to find her parents? I could ask Nathanael to help by putting her picture on the news. But that's not my call. That should be the responsibility of law enforcement. Would it be wise decision to let the general public know a child was found? Would it bring out the weirdos? Some criminal or child predator may try to take advantage of the situation by claiming Sandy. I would hate to put her in danger. Help me Lord to care for this child and keep her safe."

Kayla picked up the phone. She thought about calling Nathanael to ask for his opinion about putting an article in the paper. Then she put the phone down, "It's probably too late. It has been a long day for all of us. I'll probably see him tomorrow I'll ask him then. They had been having lunch almost every day since the run in the park.

Talitha had been questioning her about the time she's been spending with Nathanael. She tried to explain he had been such a help lately by just being there. It was a comfort for her to have someone to talk with.

Thinking about keeping Sandy safe made her think about the extortion letters she received. *"Who sent them? Why were they calling me a kidnapper? How are they connected to Sandy? And why do they think I would be willing to give them money?"*

It was difficult for Kayla to sleep even though it had been a long day. Her mind would not shut down. She kept going over the events that had happened in just a few weeks. Everything had changed. The world was not the same. She was not the same. Her friends were not the same. It was as if she stepped out of one world and into another.

In this new world she had encountered so many people that she had not met before. Some of them she just as soon she had not met them. She was familiar with DSS because of her position as teacher of young children at school. She was aware of the legal system that was in place to protect citizens. She kept abreast of the latest news the media dealt out. But now she had met them face to face and was a recipient on the opposite side of their services, the object of each establishment's investigation.

The most astonishing change is the fact that she was now the foster mother of this precocious child. She had put aside any thought of ever being a mother after the devastating episode at the orphanage. It was so traumatic, family was not allowed in her vocabulary. She wouldn't even allow herself to dream of it.

Now she is faced again with raising a child that isn't hers. It would be another devastating blow if this child is taken away too. It was too late to avoid hurt. Sandy, who was already a part of her heart, has a family out there somewhere. It is almost a certainty Sandy would be taken away.

It was a whirlwind of activity and Sandy was in the middle being pulled from all angles. Gabe, Nathanael, and people with familiar faces that kept changing were tussling with each other over Sandy. "Why are you just sitting there? Help me." Talitha was pinching her arm so tight it cut off the circulation.'

Kayla woke with a start from the disturbing dream. She had fallen asleep in her recliner and her arm was numb. She got up and checked on Sandy who was still sleeping on her bed. It was too early to get up and too late to go to bed. She did the only thing she could do. She prayed to God for peace.

CHAPTER 19

GUN IN VOLVO

All thoughts of the liquor store robbery had been put aside because more pressing matters had come up. But Eastside's evidence-holding pen had become so crowded they decided to clear up some unfinished business.

One of the items taking up space was the old Volvo. It had been headed for the crusher before Rodney and Ramon came across it at Al's junkyard. It was their misfortune and their downfall. It had blown a tire as they were fleeing from a robbery.

This case should have been easy because it involved two teens who knew very little about robbing. But since it took place across precinct lines and ended up outside the city a simple robbery turned into a 'family affair'.

Because three precincts were involved the group of officers, one from each area, decided to meet at a diner near the holding pen where the Volvo had been stowed. The case involved all three sections: Westside where the robbery took place, Eastside where Danny, the owner of the car, lived, and the sheriff department because the wreck happened outside the city limits.

When they ran a check on the plates they had found Danny Farmer was the owner. A background check showed a record of small time crimes including one of shop lifting at Sophisticates.

"I really don't think it's a coincidence that Danny's name keeps popping up when a crime has been committed," Deputy Black said as he revealed the information about the handbag incident at the mall which involved Danny and Becky. "I just had a feeling that something wasn't just right, especially since the two didn't give us their real names."

"Danny's just a small-time crook. I think it's just a coincidence that his name is on the Volvo. It was junked and sent to the junk yard. It was the two young men's misfortune to choose that one to use in a robbery. Let's to take one last look at the Volvo and send it back to the junk yard where it belongs."

I'll have a county mechanic check it out," the sheriff volunteered, "That will be one more thing we can check off our to do list."

While they were waiting, the group was still in the diner discussing some of the other cases they were working on. The strange 'found child' case on Eastside just happened to come up.

"It is odd that no one has claimed the child. At least she's with Kayla, a caring foster parent."

Rebecca from Westside thought of something and commented, "Officer Dillon isn't that about the same time you ran across Danny and Becky? Sophisticates wasn't it? If my memory serves me right both cases took place in that boutique."

As they compared notes they noticed that indeed both cases did take place at the same shop at the same time.

"Now isn't that a coincidence," Rebecca observed, "I wonder if they can be connected somehow".

"What are we looking for?" Emil asked as the sheriff walked out to the evidence holding pen where the Volvo was housed. The other officers had returned to their respective stations and were working to clear some of the other cases.

"Anything suspicious: drugs, stolen goods, burglary tools, a sack of money, etc." Sheriff Hayes grinned at his joke. "I don't really expect to find anything. It was used by two wannabe crooks, teens actually, who tried to rob a liquor store." The sheriff laughed as he remembered the case, "Their plan was doomed from the start. They went to a junk yard and rented a car so far gone it was headed for the crusher. Just as they crossed outside the city line they wrecked when a tire blew. They thought the liquor store owner was shooting at them."

The sheriff was bent over laughing as he remembered the rest. He was laughing so hard Emil started laughing as well.

"The funniest part is they rented the car for fifty dollars in exchange for fifty dollars they stole which they didn't get to keep, an old wrecked car, scratches and bruises, and a night in jail. If that didn't deter them from a life of crime I don't know what will."

The sheriff wiped his eyes as he gave Emil the instruction, "Check it out so we can declare it clean and return it to Al's Junk Yard."

Emil was glad to accept this assignment. It was the kind of task he liked. Taking things apart and putting them back together again had always fascinated him. He intended to go over every inch of it just for the heck of it.

Later that day Chief White got a call from the local bank on Eastside. It seems one of the stolen bills from O'Malley's Construction Company had been deposited in the night deposit box at their branch. It was a fifty that had been marked with a yellow highlighter. The bank deposit bag came from the local pub.

When he was questioned the bar tender he clearly remembered the bill. It came from a frequent visitor to the pub. A man by the name of Danny Farmer had come in a few days before and made a big deal about the bill being a fifty.

"He wanted to make sure I knew it was a fifty instead of a twenty," the barkeeper said. "I didn't deposit it until yesterday. I put it under the money tray because I don't have a slot for fifties I forgot all about it."

"You wouldn't believe the story of how he got the fifty. It's so weird it must be the truth. I don't think anyone would make up a story this odd and expect us to believe it," Chief White was relaying the tale to his counterparts on Westside. "He said the bill just floated down and landed at his feet."

"I think we need to jail this bird before he flees the coop," the sheriff offered as he reached to answer his cell phone.

"Okay but what charges: suspicion of robbery, murder, passing stolen bills, accessary to a crime and lying through his teeth?" Chief Whitt asked.

"Yes," was the sheriff's curt answer.

"Well would you look at this?" Emil told himself. He was so surprised at his find it took a few minutes for it to sink in. Then he called the sheriff's cell phone, "I think you need to come back out here."

"That was Emil I need to see what he wants." Sheriff Hayes called back over his shoulder as he walked out the door to see what Emil had on his mind. "Get a warrant to pick up Danny and question him about the fifty."

"The car isn't clean as you thought. Look what I found! It was in the spare tire well under a tire rim. I was about to give it a clean bill of health when something struck me as odd. Everything else was a pile of junk which had been tossed into the trunk except the tire rim. It was secured in the spare tire well where it was supposed to be," Emil held a plastic bag in his gloved hand and handed it to the sheriff. The bag contained a Luger.

"It's clearly a street gun. The identifying numbers has been filed off," the sheriff commented as he handed the gun over to another forensics team to check it out.

"There's no telling how many gangsters have handled this weapon. It's time to call the troops back together," Sheriff Hayes made the decision.

Ramon and Rodney were brought back in for questioning. Both denied having any knowledge of a gun. They were shocked to learn a gun had been found in the car.

"Either they are good actors or they in fact know nothing about the gun," the officers agreed.

"You should have seen the fear in Ramon's eyes," Rebecca felt sorry for the young man.

A detective stuck his head in the conference room, "I checked out the Volvo with DMV. Did you know Danny Farmer's name was on the title?"

"Old news," was the answer as a call came from forensics. Their Investigation showed the gun found in the Volvo was the one used in the shooting of the guard. At last credible leads were coming in.

So Danny Farmer was brought in, booked, and placed in county jail. The murder weapon was found in his car. He had possession of a bill from the armed robbery. But would this be enough to get a conviction? Hoping to find more his house was searched.

It was difficult to distinguish what was trash and what was not. It took a long time to sort through the trash and they didn't find much. The day was getting long, they were tired. What they finally ended up with was a computer, a box of newspaper clippings, letters, and a long plastic box found under the bed.

The employees at the construction company wanted to get a conviction as much as the investigators did.

While they were reviewing the surveillance tapes again, one of the regular gate guards noticed something out of order. He recognized the Black Charger.

"There it is. Run it back. Yes, that car belongs to an employee who that was fired. I remember it because the guy was always bragging especially about his expensive 'Phantom Black Pearl Dodge Charger'. See, the old decal is still on the car. I can't be sure because his face is hidden behind that hand wave but I don't think that's Joe behind the wheel."

Joe Bigalow was brought in for questioning. "I swear I didn't go back to the company. I don't have the car. I sold it. A guy I met in the bar helped me sell it."

"You mean to tell me that some guy you didn't know offered to help you sell your car?" the investigator asked.

The only thing he remembered about the guy who helped him sell the car was his name, Luther. He had a long brownish beard and mustache and always wore an old beat-up ball cap over long unkempt hair.

Sally was so proud of her car, a Dodge Charger. She had just finished cleaning it and was putting the vacuum away when Becky banged on her door crying frantically. She told her about Danny's arrest, "You should thank your lucky star you didn't keep that fifty that came out of your trunk. It was one of the bills from the robbery where the guard was killed."

She stopped her hand flew to her mouth, "Oh dear since it came from your car you may still be charged along with him." She stopped again and gulped, "And I could be held as an accessary," she wailed.

Becky was right. The police showed up at Sally's door with a warrant. She thought it was because of the fifty-dollar bill. She didn't realize the Charger was their main concern now. Since she was now the owner of the car she was served a warrant to search it. They didn't tell her much. The car was taken in and Sally was asked to accompany them for questioning.

"I don't think you'll find anything in it. I just gave it a good cleaning," she twisted her hands nervously. She hoped that wouldn't make her look guilty like she was trying to get rid of evidence.

"Sally did a good job," the mechanic admitted, "but I did found a hank of hair in a corner of the trunk stuck to the fabric. My lab expert said it was human hair with common glue on it. He made a copy of the DNA. So I guess this goes into the evidence box."

While Sally was being questioned she wondered why she was being asked more about the Charger than the fifty-dollar bill.

"So you bought the car from Fred who bought it from Joe Bigalow. And you say Joe was Hispanic." The deputy stopped and flipped through his notes to make sure.

"We talked with Joe. But he isn't Hispanic."

"Then you say some man on the phone rented the car for part of the day, but you didn't see the man. You left the keys in the car; he picked up the car at Fred's car lot and returned it to Bert's to be painted. Why did you want it painted? Was there something wrong with it? Had it been scratched or wrecked?"

The questions shocked and terrified her. She had had the car painted. Did he think she was trying to get rid of evidence? And when he repeated her words about letting someone she didn't know drive a car that was not yet hers. It didn't even sound reasonable to her.

Sally began to hyperventilate. What was happening? Was she going to be convicted of murder? The room began to swirl around her.

"Rebecca, uh Officer Stone, would you get Miss Young a glass of water and see if you can calm her down." the deputy had left the interrogation room. "She needs a breather. I think she'll do better if you finish the questioning. You seem to be better at this than I am."

Rebecca handed Sally the water and slid a mug shot of Joe across the table. "Is this the man who sold the Charger to Fred's?" she asked.

"No it doesn't even remotely resemble him. This Joe is fair and has blond hair. The Joe I met was dark skinned and had black hair."

"Okay let's get to the Volvo. Danny said you had possession of it for the last few weeks. Is that so?"

"Yes I did some work for him and that was his payment to me since I needed a car. I just never got around to transferring the car in my name."

"Then why did you buy another car?"

"That piece of junk kept breaking down. I sold it to Al's junk yard for scrap."

"Did you have tire trouble as well?"

"How did you know that? I had the mechanic who changed the tire to patch up the flat. He said it wasn't worth patching but did it anyway."

By this time Sally had recovered some of her composure. "Wait a minute. Is that the same Volvo that wrecked after a convenience store was held up? I saw it on the news. The news anchor laughed and said something about 'for the want of a tire'. I thought Old Ugly had been crushed."

Rebecca excused herself and left to check her facts with the officer. "There was no tire on the rim in the trunk of the Volvo? There were pieces of rubber that had once been a tire?"

"That's right. I was surprised when I heard Sally say the tire in the trunk had been patched. There was no patched tire in that trunk."

"So if that ridiculous story she's telling is the truth that means the patched tire had been put on the car after Sally used it and before the boys got it at Al's." Rebecca surmised.

"That's what I deduced," the fellow officer agreed.

"So someone else had a flat between the time Sally used it and the boys got it."

"If what Sally says is true a mystery man must be the one who put the gun in the tire well. But we still can't let Danny off the hook. Everything points to him."

"But Sally said someone rented the Charger and took the Volvo to the junkyard. It's got to be the truth. Who'd make up a ridiculous story like that and expect us to believe it?"

"So how much should I tell Sally? She's already plenty scared. I'd hate for her to go ballistic on us. Maybe if I calmly let her know how serious it is she will tell us more; if she knows more."

"It doesn't look good I'd hate to be in her shoes right now. She could be taking Danny's place in jail."

'I agree. It doesn't look good. I really don't think she's guilty. But Sally could be convicted on circumstantial evidence alone. She is connected to both vehicles. She had use of the Volvo which housed the Luger. She had use of the Charger that we think was used in the construction company robbery and murder. My gut feeling is she is a victim of circumstances. But gut feelings don't count in a court of law.

Sally was scared. Officer Stone left her with so many unanswered questions. "*Why are they so interested in Joe, the previous owner of the*

Charger? They say he isn't Hispanic. Then who was the man who brought the car in? Why is Danny in jail? He just had possession of a stolen fifty-dollar bill **a bill that the wind had blown out of the trunk of my car.** *Why am I not the one in jail?"* That last question terrified her.

Then her thoughts turned to Danny. What had he done? He had paid her to trail Kayla but that had nothing to do with the Charger. She felt he had something going on but she didn't concern herself with it as long as she was paid. She needed the money. When she came to show him and Becky her new car he didn't seem the least bit uneasy. That's the reason she didn't think he had anything to do with the Charger. That's what she was going to tell Rebecca Stone when she returned to question her further.

"Deputy Stone, can you tell me what's going on? Am I in trouble?" What are you looking for in my car? Sally asked, "I didn't find anything in it when I gave it a good cleaning."

"You aren't being charged with anything at the moment. All I can tell you is your two cars have been involved in crimes. Do you want to talk with a lawyer before we go on?"

That's when Sally broke down and cried. "I don't even know a lawyer if could afford one. Do you think I need one? I haven't done anything against the law so I don't see why I would need one. I don't even know what I am being charged with."

"As I said before you aren't being charged. I'm just trying to find answers to some troubling questions that just don't add up." Rebecca took out her notes, "Let me review what I have so far. Let's take the Charger first. It was sold to Fred's auto by a Joe Bigalow who according to you is Hispanic. But he isn't Hispanic. You bought the car from Fred and wanted it painted. You loved the car but hated the color. Then a man arranged over the phone to rent the car for a day and leave it at the body shop to be painted. Now let's get to the Volvo. The man on the phone was to pick up the Volvo at the body shop and carry it to the junk yard. Somewhere along the line the tire got changed. The title to this Volvo was still in Danny Farmer's name but he had given it to you as payment for a job you did for him. Is everything in my report correct so far? Is there anything else you can think of to tell me?"

"Everything in your report is correct. When you put it all together it seems preposterous. But it didn't seem so as it happened because it happened a little at a time."

"I've heard the saying, 'the truth will set you free' I'm depending on that premise." Sally prayed silently as she poured out her fears and frustration. She didn't think driving a car in someone else's name was against the law. She didn't think renting a car to a person she had not met was against the law. Last of all she had no idea the fifty-dollar bill was stolen. The wind had blown it out of the trunk and it had floated down to the ground. She was sure Danny had not seen the Charger until that unforgettable day the cursed bill landed at his feet.

"What was the job you did for Danny?"

"I watched a woman at the mall and reported to him when she left with a child."

That has nothing to do with the construction murder case," Rebecca mused, *but it sounds interesting".*

"Who was this woman?"

"Kayla Adair".

At that Rebecca's eyebrows went up. The name was familiar.

"I didn't know her name at first. He just showed me some pictures and told me to watch to see if she came out with a child." Sally was rambling again, "Then he gave me her name when he asked me to deliver a basket to her at school. I thought that was a sweet thing to do. At first I thought he had a thing for her but his girlfriend didn't seem to mind. So I must have been mistaken. It must have been he felt sorry for her because some reporter printed a terrible picture of her in the newspaper. I was there when he saw the picture. Boy did he get mad but I didn't ask questions. You don't ask Danny questions when he's angry. Don't get me wrong. Danny has his faults but he's no killer."

Sally had noticed Rebecca's reaction when she mentioned Kayla's name. She didn't want to say anything to get Danny in trouble but she didn't want to implicate herself either. *"I just watched Kayla and reported to Danny. I hope watching a person isn't against the law."*

Danny was still not of the hook even though he didn't match the description given by the two witnesses. He was the only suspect they had. So Rebecca decided to go back over the evidence taken from Danny's house. There was nothing except his computer and the flat plastic box found under his bed which contained pictures of a woman.

CHAPTER 20

KAYLA'S CAR HIJACKED

Kayla belted Sandy in the back seat on the passenger side. This was one of the precautions she took after being awarded temporary custody of Sandy. She had seen on the news about a wreck where a child was killed when the driver was thrown against a child sitting in a car seat in the back. It took a little more time but if it saved the child it was worth it. She had opened the front door of the passenger side to let the car cool off while she buckled her in.

A man rushed up to her, snatched the keys out of her hand, and shoved her aside. He ran around to get in on the driver's side as Kayla stumbled to her feet and jumped in to lock the doors. But he was already in the car. As he put the car in drive, she frantically reached for the keys. But he knocked her hand away.

"Get out!" he yelled and tried to shove her out.

"No!" she yelled back as he floorboarded the car.

"Look Lady I don't want to hurt you, I just need your car," He tried to explain as he barreled out of the parking lot.

"But my baby's in the back seat! Let me get her! Let us out! You can have the car!"

"A baby, Damn! I thought you were putting groceries in. Nobody puts a baby on that side."

"Well I do! Just let us out!"

"I can't. That'd take too much time. Time I don't have. Now just shut up and let me concentrate on driving, unless you want us to wreck."

123

"Boy I know how to pick them, a woman with a baby!" he muttered as he relived the last few minutes. He was in the store getting a pack of cigarettes. He had run out. His nerves were shot; he needed a smoke. So he chanced a run to the store. When the policeman headed straight for him with his hand resting on the gun at his hip, he ran out the back door and across the road to the grocery. He didn't have time to think. He just hijacked the first car he came to. If the policeman found the gun in his waistband he would be headed to jail. He couldn't let that happen. Then they'd find out what he did. He'd get the death sentence for sure. He needed to get out of town, out of the country.

"He was going to shoot me. I could see it in his eyes. When he yelled for me to stop, I had no choice. I had to run."

He didn't realize he said it out loud until she asked, "Who was going to shoot you?"

Back at the convenience store the policeman reached over and helped the woman untangle her purse strap from the shelf that almost toppled over on her. He had not seen the man run out the back door.

They were traveling on the interstate keeping up with traffic flow which was over the speed limit. It was difficult to keep his speed in check. But he didn't want to bring attention to himself by going too slow or too fast.

Kayla desperately tried to think what to do. She didn't know if it would be better to keep talking or be quiet. She could tell he was a bundle of nerves.

"Where are you going?" It just slipped out. She couldn't keep herself from asking. She was as scared as he was.

"I don't know! I just have to keep moving. Look, it's not like I planned this trip it just happened, okay?" he answered sharply.

His tone caused Kayla to stop talking. She didn't want to agitate him. She was unsure what he might do.

"This thing is digging in my back," he muttered as he calmly pulled the pistol from his back and stuck it in his waistband in front. He didn't notice the shock on her face.

"He has a gun! Dear God," she prayed, *"Help us. Give me some direction. Tell me what to do."*

After thirty minutes he couldn't stand the silence, "Okay, I don't know where we're going."

Kayla jumped when he broke the silence. She had been deep in prayer. "I'm sorry. Were you asleep? I didn't mean to wake you."

"No I wasn't sleeping" Kayla noticed the change in his disposition.

"It's too quiet. I can't think straight with all this silence."

He was a gregarious man. He used this outgoing trait to his advantage. It helped him in and out of situations. But this was one hole he didn't know if he could ever dig himself out of.

"I even talk to myself sometimes. I guess you noticed that."

"Yes." Even with the change she didn't know what to do. Was he the kind of person who lost his temper easily? Would she say something to spark it again?

"*Lord Jesus, tell me what to do,*" she started praying again, "*Sandy and I need your protection. But this man must be in deep trouble. He said somebody wants to shoot him. He needs Your help as well. He wants to talk but what do I say?*" She remembered the gun and decided to keep quiet.

"If you're not sleeping what are you doing?" he asked as he noticed she kept closing her eyes.

"*Okay God I'm trusting on You to give me the words to say.*"

"I'm not sleeping I'm praying."

"Praying?"

"*There's that tone back. He's upset again. Well, let him be upset.*"

"What do you expect? You hijack me and my baby. You tried to shove me out of my own car. You're speeding down the interstate but you don't know where you're going. You said somebody was going to shoot you. And you have a gun. Yes, I saw the gun. Yes, I'm praying. What would you do in this situation, shoot somebody?" she didn't mean to raise her voice but she was annoyed.

"*Oh boy I did it now. Why did I say that? Sometimes I don't wait for God to give me the words. I just take it on myself. He could just shoot us and we'd be out of his hair. He only wants the car anyway.*"

"*This woman is some piece of work. I saw the fear on her face. Now she's furious. She does have a right to be mad.*" He couldn't help but smile.

"Oh, you're one of those 'holy rollers'. So what were you asking God to do? Cause me to have a heart attack and get you out of this predicament?"

"I am a Christian but I don't consider myself a 'holy roller'. And I didn't ask God to harm you. I asked God to protect us. You are one of the 'us' I was asking God to help.

"Me? I don't need …"

"Who am I kidding? Look at me, the more I try to get out this mess the deeper I get."

The look on his face told her it was God who had given her the right words.

"Don't get me wrong. There's nothing wrong with what you call 'holy rollers'. There are a lot of different kinds of churches and denominations. We worship the same God, just in different ways." She didn't want to give him the wrong impression. She had nothing against the other denominations.

"So what kind are you?" He asked. This topic was just as good as any since she wasn't preaching at him. She was just explaining differences.

She wasn't afraid any more. She didn't seem to be in danger. He wanted to chat. Maybe God's hand was in this from the beginning.

Four hours later the gas gauge began to ping. They had only fifty more miles on the tank of gas. They had driven almost four hundred miles. The two adults had settled into quiet nonthreatening conversation. Neither of them wanted to bring up the situation they were in. Sandy slept most of the time. When she was awake she was content with the snacks Kayla had given her.

The snacks were left over from the trip to the community recreation park. They had packed a picnic lunch and stayed until the park closed. Sandy had enjoyed all the park had to offer. She played with the other children at the slides and swings, fed the animals, and splashed around in the pool. By this time both Sandy and Kayla were exhausted. On the way home Kayla decided to stop by the grocery to pick up snacks. The impromptu outing had depleted their supply at home. They were in the store longer than planned because Kayla decided to pick up a few other items as well. It was dusk when they reached the car. That's when hijacking took place.

They would be totally out of gas in fifty miles. He had to do something. When he saw a Gas Express sign he pulled off. This was a place where he could pay cash there at the pump.

He pointed at her with the gun, "You stay in the car," he instructed. He slid several bills through the slot at the window and filled the tank with gas.

"I could have used my cell phone while he was pumping gas but I don't have it." Kayla was still trying to think of a way to escape. She left her purse at home on purpose. It would be just another thing to keep up with. So she took a few dollars and only what she needed for a picnic. *"I forgot to get my phone out of my purse. How was I to know I would be abducted?"*

"I must be slipping I should have taken her cell phone." He chastised himself as he got back in the car. *"I didn't see her use a phone. Everybody has a cell phone these days. I don't even see her purse. It must be in the back seat."*

"Mommy I have to go," Sandy declared as she twisted around and stretched her arms. She had been asleep in the seat for hours and needed to stretch.

"I'll pull off at the next rest area. If no one is there we'll stop, if you promise not to try anything." He waited for an answer.

"Okay, I promise!"

"I know rest areas aren't always safe so you two do your business, I'll make a quick run and be right back out to keep watch. Wait, empty your pockets."

"I keep my promises," Kayla huffed as she pulled out a change purse and handed it to him. She patted the pockets of her shorts to show there wasn't anything else in them.

While he waited he got snacks and water from the vending machines. He used all the small bills he had. So he opened her change purse to see if she had any. It contained a few bills and her driver's license. *"Kayla Adair, why does that name ring a bell?"*

"Even if I didn't make that promise what can I do? I can't even write on the mirror with lipstick. I don't have any with me. Even if I did, what good would it do? We'd be five hundred miles down the road before anyone saw it," Kayla shrugged.

He was getting tired and the constant hum of the car was making him sleepy. He had been driving all night. They were in the middle of nowhere so he thought it would be safe to stop and rest. He pulled off on the interstate and drove several miles on an old two lane country road. The pot holes in the road indicated the paved part had not been maintained in a while but it was passable because the shoulders had been freshly mowed and bushes trimmed back. A mixture of conifers and hardwoods lined the road with patches of wasteland in between.

The sun was just peeking over the horizon when he spotted an old rusted sign. It was skewed; one side barely hanging on. The only thing keeping it on the post was a honeysuckle vine and one bent rusty nail. The other side didn't fare so well. He almost missed it because of the tall weeds surrounding it. Most of the words had weathered away. He could only make out two words 'youth camp'. He turned on the road leading to the camp. He could tell at one time it had been paved. But now it was more like a path. Patches of tall grass and weeds grew in the cracks. Pale green wild plumb bushes and patches of smoky gray berry bushes were taking possession of the unused land along the roadside. A grove of tall slender trees stood a short distance away. The scenery gave him a temporary sense of peace. It was wild but beautiful.

The sound of briars scraping against the side of her car woke Kayla up. "What are you doing?"

"Following this road," he answered as if it was nothing out of the ordinary.

He came to a stop at the end of the road.

"What is this?" Kayla asked as she looked around at the ramshackle buildings.

"The sign said a youth camp, I think."

There were several buildings on the site in different stages of disintegration. A large block building dominating most of the area sat in the middle of the compound. Well-worn cabins sat along the perimeter of the grounds. A bathhouse separated the cabins into two groups. Kayla could almost hear the echoes of laughing children as they raced about near the cabins. But now the steps they used to enter the cabins were now piles of rotting wood scattered in front of sagging doors. Years of neglect had allowed the activities area to be taken over by yard debris. Broken rusting pieces of abandoned playground equipment was scattered about.

"Well, we're home," he announced as he stood in the midst of the rubble with his arms outstretched.

As he lifted his arms Kayla caught sight of the gun in his waistband. That brought her back to reality. They had not spoken of their dilemma in a while. It was like an unspoken agreement.

"I don't care much for your sense of humor," she groused as she got out and looked around.

"Don't you like it? We're at summer camp."

"Mommy, I want out too. I want to see the camp," came from the back seat.

They were careful to watch their step as they walked around. They found the largest building still intact. It was a cement block building which seemed to be the dining hall. The windows were boarded up and the front and back metal doors were still closed tight.

He started searching around the building looking under rocks and poking in cracks.

"What are you doing now?"

"I'm searching for a spare key. There's always a spare key hidden for emergencies." He answered.

"Now where could that key be? He asked himself. "I don't usually have this much trouble finding the spare key." He stood with his hand on his chin thinking out loud. He decided they all needed a day or two and rest. This was as good a place as any. There didn't seem to be anyone on his trail yet.

Kayla stood around watching him search then decided to check out the place. A small metal plaque on the wall at the front door piqued her interest. On it was an etching depicting Jesus with the words, 'Key to the kingdom'.

"That's right. He is the key," She agreed as she studied the tarnished plaque. She rubbed it to shine it up and felt a slight wobble. It was so subtle she thought she might have imagined the movement.

"How fitting and clever," she said with a smile as she reached out and nudged the etching. It seemed to move a little so she nudged it again. It pivoted on a tiny pin that appeared to be part of the etching. "There's the key."

Because the flap over the keyhole protected it from the weather the key worked. But when they tried to open the door, the rusted hinges would not give.

"I have cooking oil in the car I bought it at the grocery where you hij ... uh ... Let's try that." Kayla suggested as she headed for the car.

They poured oil on the hinges but the door still would not budge.

"Why don't we let it soak? What else do you have in the car?" he asked as he remembered she had been shopping at the grocery store. "I hope you have something better to eat than cooking oil."

If not he hoped the two bottles of water and left over snacks from what he bought at the rest area would last two days.

"Lucky for you, I was hungry when I was shopping. I have bread and luncheon meat." She opened the trunk and pulled an antibacterial wipe out of the dispenser and washed her and Sandy's hands. Before she could put the wipe in a trash bag he took it from her and wiped his own hands. She took plastic plates from the basket and sandwich makings out of the cooler and made each one a sandwich.

He was about to pick up the sandwich and take a bite when Sandy reached for his hand and took Kayla's, "Mommy, it's my time."

"Okay go ahead, Sweety," she answered as she bowed her head.

"Thank you Jesus for the sandwich and milk. I like it but I don't like this place. Please don't let Mr. Man get mad at Mommy again. Amen."

He was taken aback and didn't know what to say so he ate in silence. He gained composure as he helped put the leftover food away.

"You seem to be prepared for every emergency. Do you always carry a cooler in your trunk?"

"Not usually but we spent the day at the park and I carried a picnic lunch in the cooler. It came in handy when I went to get groceries. And since I have S ... a child, I keep wipes handy."

"Look at us we have food to eat, water to drink, and a place to stay. What else could a person want?"

"Water to wash in, electricity, a bathroom, clean clothes, and a soft bed with clean linen, to name a few."

They tried the door again but it still stubbornly resisted.

"I'm going to look around to see if I can find something to use to help jar the hinge. You stay here. It's not safe to be wondering around in this junk. And you never know what might slither out from under a rock."

Is he talking about an animal or himself? Okay Lord I know that wasn't a very nice thing to think. If he got a decent haircut, trimmed that scruffy beard, and got rid of that tatty baseball hat he wouldn't look so bad.

He found a hammer in the tool shed. He also brought out a rake and bowsaw he found. "If I use some oil on the saw, I might be able to clean some of the bushes from around the door."

The hammer did the trick. After a few whacks the hinge gave up and the door opened.

The people in charge of camp maintenance had done a good job winterizing the building since it was open only in the summer. Metal storage cabinets kept rats from gnawing holes and getting to the contents. Even the vents had been plugged to keep out varmints.

It was dark inside since the windows had been shored up with boards. They pulled boards off two windows to let in light. Kayla found a broom in one of the cabinets and started sweeping the floor near the window that was letting in light. *"Sandy needs a place to run and play. She can't stay in the car all day. The area is so overgrown with weeds and riddled with debris she can't play outside."*

"I don't think that's a very good idea."

Kayla jumped when he spoke, "What?" She was deep in her thoughts as she went about cleaning a spot for Sandy and didn't hear him approach.

"You're stirring up too much dust," he said after Sandy started sneezing. "Does she have a respiratory problem like asthma or allergies?" That's the last thing he wanted. If she had an asthma attack she could die before they got her to a hospital. He tried to shake off the memory of the little girl.

"I don't know. Uh... I don't think so. Uh... Okay I'll stop sweeping. I was just trying to fix a clean place to play in." She stammered.

"That's odd. She doesn't know if her own child has allergies."

He took the broom, sprinkled water on it, and brushed off one of the wooden tables. It was long and made of thick rough lumber. The legs were four by fours and the top was made of two by six boards.

"This thing is heavy", he said as he hefted one end of the table. "Here help me shove it against the wall."

"Get some of those towels from the cabinet and spread them on the table," he directed. "That should be more comfortable than the cement floor anyway."

He went to the car and brought back the picnic blanket and put it on the towels Kayla had spread out.

"I think we should bring the cooler in here," he said as he headed back to the car. He was glad the cooler was one of the expensive kinds that kept food cold for a long time.

He returned with the cooler, a pillow, and a plastic box. "As I said before, you sure are prepared for emergencies. I found this squeezed in the space beside the spare tire." He said as he opened the box and pulled out a tightly rolled tarp and windbreaker. "What's this for?"

"I keep it in the trunk in case I have a flat or something. You never know when it might come in handy. The pillow is for S ...uh... the baby."

"I may as well bring in the rest of the groceries. We can use the tarp to wrap them in to keep out bugs, spiders, and such that might be creeping around." He watched her face hoping to get a reaction.

"Sounds good to me," was her calm reaction.

Milk, small bottles of juice, luncheon meat, sandwich spread, and a container of fruit were in the cooler. He brought in bags containing dry cereal, bread, a jar of peanut butter and jelly and paper towels. The picnic basket held chips, pickles, plastic utensils, napkins, and bottles of water. Under his arm was the container of antibacterial wipes.

"We could camp here for a month!"

"I'm going to clean out a spot outside for her to play," he left with the rake and saw, "This place is too grungy, she doesn't need to be breathing all this dust. She's already sneezing."

"And I'll scout around and see what else I can find."

He found a storage building housing mattresses stacked against a wall.

The plastic covered mattresses were full of holes and rat's nests. He found one in the middle of the stack that seemed free of holes. He pulled it out and let it fall with a thwack onto the floor. He lifted it up and dropped it several times to rid it of as much dust as he could. He hoisted it on his shoulders and carried it to the dining hall and he went back for another one.

An earsplitting scream pierced the air.

"What happened?" Kayla's jerked awake and almost fell off the table she and Sandy were sleeping on. Her eyes flew open but she peered into the darkness.

Something had crawled across his face. He flicked his lighter and saw a mouse scurrying as best he could on three legs. As it scrambled it was being pulled in a circle by the limp fourth leg.

"The poor thing it must have been in your mattress and you smushed it. Is he one of the creepy crawly things you were talking about?" she laughed.

"Smushed is not a word."

"Sounds good to me. It fits don't you think?"

"I'm going outside," he grumbled.

The moonlight was enough for him to find limbs and twigs he had raked in a pile. "I need some s'mores." He said as he sat near the fire. He had heard that was what campers ate around a campfire.

"Mind if we join you?" Kayla and Sandy came out wrapped in the blanket.

Kayla was no longer afraid of him. *"He's an enigma. Maybe it's because he's as meticulous as I am when it comes to cleaning up."* After each meal he had helped clean the plastic palates and utensils with wipes and burned the paper trash. *"We've been here three days and I haven't thought about trying to get away. Of course where would we go if we did try to leave? We're in the wilderness and I don't even know where the nearest town is."*

His kindness reminded her of Gabe. *"I really miss that man. I didn't realize how much I depended on him until lately. I thought he was going to kiss me for sure the day the police came to question me. Darn it! They could have waited a few minutes longer!"*

Thinking about the kiss made her remember Nathanael's. That one was cut short as well. They were watching a movie and she forgot about her standing date with Gabe. She remembered only after Nathanael mentioned it was Friday.

"This is getting confusing. I need to get my mind off both of them." She had been thinking of the situation for a while.

"I wonder what's happening back home."

He jumped as Kayla broke the silence. This was their third breakfast. He was wondering what to do. They were getting low on provisions and couldn't stay there much longer.

"Why don't we listen to the news on the radio in the car? It should come on at noon, don't you think?"

There wasn't much on the news. There were few leads coming in about the construction company murder robbery case. Danny Farmer was still the only suspect at the time. There was nothing, no news about them. Even though he really didn't want to be arrested it was still a disappointment. It was as if they had been forgotten. No one cared. What about his two hostages? No alerts for either for them. Didn't they matter?

"We'll try again tonight."

He noticed their supply of food and water was almost depleted. "I need to go a store. It's probably safe to venture out since no alert has been issued," he decided.

CHAPTER 21

SANDY & KAYLA MISSING

"Kayla, I haven't heard from you in several days." Talitha left the message. She and Kayla usually talked every day. She waited for an answer.

That's not like Kayla. She usually answers right back even if she has something else to do. But after an hour she decided to text her. "I guess you and Sandy have been doing you own thing. See you tomorrow morning."

"Get the pancake batter ready I'll be there in ten minutes," Talitha texted her Saturday morning. There had been no answer yet from her other texts. Now she was beginning to worry.

No one was home when Talitha got there. Kayla's car was not in the garage. She called again. All her calls went to voice mail.

"Gabe have you seen Kayla lately?" her cell phone was held to her ear with her shoulder as she called him and used her key to get in.

"No she promised not to forget our Friday night out again, but she didn't show. I thought she must've had her mind on Sandy."

"I'm at her house now and her car's gone. We always have breakfast together on Saturdays. I can't imagine what could have happened. She didn't call to let me know she wouldn't be home. That just is not like Kayla."

"I'm calling her right now!" Gabe began to worry as well.

"I found her phone," Talitha answered Kayla's phone. "It was in her purse in her bedroom."

"I'm coming over," Gabe ran to his car and rushed over.

"How long have they been missing?" Sheriff Hayes asked.

"I talked with her on Monday," Tabitha answered, "I haven't heard from her since."

"So you don't know if she's really missing. You just haven't heard from her in a few days. She has to be gone for two days before we fill out a missing person's report."

Gabe looked at Talitha, "I don't know what else to do. I hate to include Nathanael but we may need his help." He finally had to admit he was jealous of the time Kayla had spent with him.

"Nathanael, it's Lilly. I just heard over the scanner that something's going on over at Miss Adair's. She and Sandy may be missing. I thought you might want to see if there's a story there."

"I know I just got a call from Gabe Elder." He didn't want to say anything else because Lilly had a tendency to think the worse especially when it came to Kayla.

He was right Lilly contacted a rookie reporter who was more than willing to check it out.

"This might be one way to get my foot in the door." The rookie thought to herself as she rang the doorbell. No one answered. But the sheriff's car was parked in front and two cars were in the driveway. She hated to leave the scene without some kind of story. She noticed a woman across the street dressed in a house coat and slippers with her hand above her eyes shading out the bright sun. She was intent on watching the proceedings even though nothing was happening outside.

"She looks like a likely candidate to share news," she told herself as she went over to talk with the neighbor.

"How long has Miss Adair and the child been missing," the reporter asked.

The neighbor perked up when she heard the news. She was glad to finally learn what was going on and agreed to talk.

"This is a live report from in front of Kayla Adair's house. We just received an unofficial report that a child known only as Sandy is missing. She may be in the company of Miss Adair. As you may recall this is the same Kayla Adair that was in the news a few weeks ago. You can see the sheriff's car behind me parked in her driveway. I've been speaking with the neighbor across the street." she said toward the news camera then turned to the neighbor. "How long have you known Miss Adair?" The reporter asked as she pointed the mike in the neighbor's face.

"I haven't met her yet. I moved here just before she was arrested in April for kidnapping. You said they are missing? I hope she hasn't taken another child."

"The sheriff has no comment at this time."

The sheriff had crossed the street to talk with the neighbor and motioned to the reporter to cut the interview.

"Has another child been kidnapped?" the neighbor asked before the sheriff had a chance to speak.

He ignored the question, "When was the last time you saw Miss Adair?"

"I saw her a few days ago, she was putting something in the trunk of her car. I couldn't see much because she had backed her car up to the door. The front was facing me. It could've been a suitcase. She made several trips to the car."

"Do you remember what they were wearing?"

"Oh yes, Miss Adair was wearing green shorts and a white tee with a green flower to match the shorts. The child was wearing a playsuit covered with pink flowers. She was carrying a pink backpack.

"What am I going to do with my two companions? We could leave this place but where would we go? I need to do some serious thinking. I'd be better off if the baby had not been in the back, if the mother had not jumped in the car." They needed food and water. No one was looking for them so he thought it would be safe to go out for provisions.

Several miles down the highway he noticed a 'Welcome to Mesa Verde' sign and Express Gas advertisement. He took the exit and pulled up to the gas pump.

"I may as well fill up while we're here. Stay in the car!" He demanded as he went inside. He was paying the cashier when his hand stopped in midair. Kayla and Sandy's picture appeared on the TV.

"… child, … missing, … company of Miss Kayla Adair, … kidnapped another child, … sheriff," That's all he heard as he bolted out and pumped the gas.

"We have to hurry. Get a change of clothes. I'll pick up some food and water," he muttered the order as he quickly ushered them into the Expressway Dollar Store. "I hope you have some money I'm running out."

Kayla put a few items for Sandy on the counter, "Kidnapped." She whispered.

"Si," was his smiling reply.

"Abducted," she tried again.

"Si," he smiled again.

"Mommy what is abducted?" Sandy asked.

"Shhhh," she whispered as she led her to another section of the store. *"Lord what are You doing to me here?"*

Everyone was quiet on the trip back to the camp. He was thinking about the news report. She was wondering if he had heard what she said to the clerk.

"So you're the woman who kidnapped that child at the mall." He had waited until Sandy was asleep. They were sitting near the campfire and he wanted to get some answers.

"How did you?" she began.

"Your pictures were splashed across the TV in the gas station. Some woman said she hoped you had not kidnapped another child. What kind of person are you? You're no better than I am," he accused her.

"What makes you say that? Have I said or done anything to give you the impression I think I'm better than you? Well, you're right. I'm not better than you, in God's sight that is. We all are His children if we want to be. But I'm no kidnapper."

"Here we go again talking about God. What does God have to do with any of this? You're a kidnapper? Does God condone kidnapping?"

*"Who am I to talk? I'm a thief and murderer **and a kidnapper**."*

"So he wants to talk again. But he wants to talk about me. What about him? I don't know a thing about him. Well he hasn't harmed us so far so here goes."

"God has everything to do with it. He's my protector, The One I go to for guidance and strength. And no I don't think God overlooks kidnapping but He does forgive sins."

"Where was He when I stole your car with you and your ...uh ... the child?"

"I don't pretend to know all the answers. I don't know why He allowed us to be hijacked by you. It was nothing I did. I didn't make that choice. We were just in the wrong place at the wrong time when you decided to take a car. But you made the choice. There is a difference. All I know is

He helps me get through trying days. He can help you too. You must be in trouble. If not why did you hijack my car? Why do you carry a gun? What have you done to make someone want to shoot you? And as I said before I'm not a kidnapper."

"Then why are you being called a kidnapper on the news?" He still wasn't convinced.

"Well he didn't lose his temper but he didn't answer my question either."

"It's a long story, one you may not believe."

"I have all night. I'll be the judge of that after I hear what you have to say."

"I'll start with the evening I met Sandy. That's what I call her. I'm Kayla by the way, but I guess you know that now."

"I was in my own little world, safe in my little space, content to let life carry me along like a gentle breeze when this little hand reached up and took mine. Everything has been turned upside down since then."

It was well into the night when she finished. He listened attentively and occasionally asked questions.

"Wow! That's some story. I don't know if I believe you or not. You say you still don't know who she is or why she came to you?"

"That's right I don't know anything about her except what I observed during the time she has been with me. She's very intelligent but insists I am her mother."

"That's enough about me. Now it's your time. You have evaded all of my questions. You may as well tell me what kind of trouble you're in. What do you have to lose?"

"My story is just as unbelievable as yours. Mine is a mixture of coincidences and circumstances that keep getting worse. I try not to think about it. That's the reason I keep talking about other things. It terrifies me."

"It may help to talk about it. It might not be as scary as you think."

"So the child's name is Sandy and you're Kayla Adair. You can call me Luther."

"Okay Luther, you're evading again. Get it out in the open. Things don't seem so bad in the light of day."

"I'm afraid daylight will only show how much trouble I'm in. No one will believe it was an accident."

CHAPTER 22

LUTHER' STORY

The chair creaked as Luther leaned back the broken recliner. He was at home trying to think of a way to get his hands on some fast money. He was still short of cash.

As he sat there mulling over his lack of funds, his mind went back to Joe and some of his ramblings. Luther had listened to Joe's whining about his fate. It wasn't **his** fault that he was fired. It wasn't **his** fault he still owed for the car. That was one thing about Luther he was a patient listener. When he was still a boy he had learned the hard way, it was better to listen. He had learned a lot by just listening.

He remembered the first time he laid eyes on Joe. His last job had not netted him half as much as he had been promised by his fence. So there he was sitting at the bar brooding over his lack of funds. Joe stomped in letting the door slam behind him, slapped his fist on the counter, and ordered a beer. The bartender told him to take his beer and attitude over to a table in a far corner. Luther decided to take advantage of the opportunity. He picked up his drink, sidled over to Joe, and struck up a conversation. Over the course of the next few days Luther and Joe found themselves in the same bar at the same table, comrades of a sort, chitchatting about the unfairness of life. Joe, however, did most of the talking.

As Joe talked he shared his problems with Luther. Not only had he lost his job but he owed money to a loan shark. He had borrowed money from a loan shark to buy an expensive car. He just had to have the 'Phantom Black Pearl Dodge Charger'. He was in trouble. Not only was he about to lose the car, he was afraid of what might happen to him.

Another lesson Luther had learned as a boy is sometimes it pays to help others. So Luther decided to help Joe sell his car. It wouldn't cost him anything to help Joe. He knew people. He had contacts besides that, some of Joe's rambling sparked an interest. Maybe he could use some of the facts he threw out as he ranted. If he helped Joe sell the car he may keep talking.

As he recalled parts of the conversations of those last a few days, a plan began to formulate. He popped the recliner to a sitting position and began to concentrate. His mind began to focus on details of Joe's comments. The rest of the day he planned. It took a few weeks to do the preliminary ground work and set his plans in motion. His habit of listening was about to pay off.

So Luther the thief woke early because his job today was to hold up a construction company. They would not be expecting it. No one holds up a construction company.

Luther looked in the mirror and checked out his outfit. Several shirts had been discarded as unacceptable. He especially liked the gray one with a mountain scene. It was his lucky shirt. But he needed to wear a nondescript one. He needed to blend in with the normal crowd. He would enter the facility wearing work clothes as a normal construction worker. Then he would transform himself into a businessman.

In preparation he had let his beard grow longer than his usual stubble. A barber friend styled his hair and beard to fit the businessman look. He glued his own discarded hair to his old scruffy ball cap. He would use this after the robbery to reverse the transformation back to the old Luther until his own hair grew back.

He was dressed as a normal construction worker. He took a stiff hair brush and dabbed a little boot black on his face to make him appear to have a two day shadow. He placed a briefcase, a bag with a change of clothes, and his makeup supplies in the trunk of Joe's Charger.

He planned to enter the maintenance building again this morning but he would not pull the robbery until most of the employees were at lunch. He had done his homework. He had spent a lot of time listening to Joe ramble. But some of his ramblings revealed tidbits he could use. He learned from Joe the security guard ate his lunch early and usually took an after lunch nap about that time.

He knew the routine of the workers there. He had checked out the route of the armored car. It brought the wages on Thursday and the workers were paid on Friday. The two women in charge of payments would be sorting out the salaries on Thursday during lunch time because there were less people around to interrupt the job. He knew the layout of the business. He had worked hard on his plans and today it would pay off. Today he was going to collect 'his salary'.

A surprise met him when he arrived at the front gate. His confidence slipped a bit when he saw the regular guard had been replaced. Luther should have done a lot more research. Since this was Spring Break for schools, several workers were on vacation. He should have listened to his instincts that told him to back out but he didn't. He had put too much work and planning to let it go.

He was driving the Charger with Joe's company pass still attached to the windshield. He had arranged to borrow the Charger from Sally. He was lucky to get it just before she had it painted. The plan began to formulate when Joe groused about O'Malley's Construction Company. Now the plan was coming together. He didn't worry about getting in because he had no trouble getting in before when he checked out the place.

The hairs on the back of his neck rose when he saw that the guard vigorously checking out the car in front of him. It was too late he couldn't back out now. After waiting in line to enter he was committed. It would look suspicious if he turned around now. He reached over and got the Joe's badge out of his hard hat. While he waited he pinned the badge on his shirt in a conspicuous place and put the hard hat on his head.

The other times he had glided through with the Charger which still had the company pass. A smile, a nod, a wave of his hand and he was in.

He felt a sense of smugness as he was waved in. He reveled in the fact he had the ability to adjust to the situation.

"*A piece of cake,*' he said to himself as he waved his hand just in time to block out the focus of the security camera.

"*So there was a changing of the guard. Just a little glitch in my plans,*" Luther thought to himself as he patted his chest where his lucky shirt should have been. Then he remembered changing into a less conspicuous shirt. He was not wearing his lucky shirt but not to worry things were going quite well without it.

As he drove to the parking lot in the back he mentally checked his list: dress shirt, sports jacket, tie and don't forget loafers, work-boots would be a total give away. So he backed the car in a parking space next to the wall, quickly changed into his business attire, removed the boot black from his face with the tissue he had prepared with lotion, and grabbed the briefcase from the trunk. As he was about to close the trunk lid he spied his pistol in the trunk and without thinking he stuck it in the briefcase. Then he thought about the gun as he walked into the administration building.

"Maybe I was meant to bring it. Those ladies may be more willing to give up the money bag with a little persuasion on my side. Would you just listen to me? I can't believe what a change of clothes does to a person." He laughed at himself, *"With my knock-about clothes on I would have said, 'The old broads would be happy to hand over the loot.'."*

So with this jovial attitude Luther the thief disengaged the locked door, walked into the office, pulled out the gun, and announced, "Ladies I'm going to relieve you of this tedious job of counting out the salaries." He opened the briefcase, "If you would be kind enough to place the money in here I'll be out of your way, after I lock you in the closet that is."

Except for the little glitch at the front gate everything seemed to be falling into place just as Luther had planned. He had just locked the women in the closet when suddenly his plans fell apart. A guard rushed in and the gun in Luther's hand went off. Everything went haywire.

He hadn't realized this was spring break week. Because school was out some workers were on family vacations.

This was the case of the regular guard. He was using the spring break to go on vacation with his family. Therefore there was a different guard watching the front office. And this guard did not take an after-lunch nap. This guard was on guard. This guard saw Luther on the surveillance camera. He saw Luther jimmy the lock on the office door. He yelled into his mike alerting his fellow guards. But they were too far away to reach the office.

It all happened so fast it seemed unreal. Luther was startled when the guard rushed into the room. He reacted without thinking. The gun in his hand went off striking the guard. He was in shock as he threw the gun in the briefcase with the money and ran.

Luther, small time drug dealer, gun runner, carjacker, and all around thief did not intend to shoot anyone. He was a thief. That was his job. He was just doing his job. The only job he had ever known. He was Luther. His only name was Luther. He was just Luther.

Back at his flat the shaken Luther couldn't help but relive the scene. It was as if the gun had taken a life of its own. It had gone off by itself. It had happened so fast he didn't have time to think he just went through the motions. Since he had rehearsed the escape he didn't have to think. He had managed to get through the deliveries gate at the back entrance before it was locked down. Joe had told him it was not unusual for haulers to park their big rigs there and go home in a personal car.

He paced the floor trying to calm his nerves. "*That was a close call. They almost caught me. I barely got changed back into my work clothes and out the back gate. Thank you Joe for telling me about the back gate where deliveries come in. Thank goodness he told me about that exit.*"

He needed to think what to do next. Killing the guard was not part of his plans. It was an accident. He was not a killer he was just a thief. He was not a bad person who took from the poor. He only took from those who had more than they knew what to do with. He was distraught as he sat down on the bed with his bowed head in his hands he raked his fingers through his hair trying to think. It didn't work. He couldn't think. The room was mess. He had left his clothes scattered on the bed and chair. He hated clutter. He couldn't think with clutter all over the room. So he rose from the room and started picking up his clothes and putting the room in order.

As he worked he tried to settle his nerves. "I didn't mean to shoot the gun. I only carried it in to scare the women. How did I know the guard would rush in and startle me? It was an accident."

Luther started pacing again. He flung his arms back and forth as walked from the bedroom through the living area to the kitchen and back to the bedroom. He started hitting his right fist in his left hand as he paced, "Okay, okay, what's done is done. I have to calm down so I can think straight. He sat down at the kitchen table and jumped back up, "I can't just sit down and hope things will blow over. I've got better sense than that. But what do I do now?"

As he talked to himself he lifted his forefinger in the air. "The first thing I have to do is return Sally's Charger to the fix-it shop." Then he enumerated the rest of the things he needed to do, "Pick up the Volvo, take it to the junk yard, get rid of the gun, and stash away the money." He couldn't believe he had held onto the briefcase as he made his escape.

"First order of business, return the car. Return the Charger, how am I going to do that?" he asked himself out loud.

His thoughts returned to the botched robbery. He had covered all bases. He had cased the place out. He had used Joe's car to gain entrance. He knew the routine of the guard. He checked the grounds and timed his getaway. He couldn't believe all his plans went haywire just because the guards had been changed.

He tried to think of what he needed to do next. But his brain wouldn't let go. He kept going over the plans he had made. While he was in the process of planning the robbery he thought he had covered every aspect.

He would use Joe's Charger with the company decal on it to get through the gate. He told Joe he needed to show the car off to potential buyers. But instead he used the Charger to gain entrance when he checked the place out. Then he talked Jose' into carrying the Charger to Fred's Used Car Lot.

After the Charger was sold to Fred's he remembered he needed the company decal one more time.

"That was stupid of me. I should have kept it another week," he admonished himself.

He called Fred's Car Lot.

"Fred's Used Cars Sally speaking," a woman answered.

"*Great. Just the woman I wanted to talk with,*" thought Luther.

"I'd like to speak with someone about a black Charger you have."

Jose' told him how much Sally liked the car and how determined she was to get it. She loved the car except for the black metallic paint. She told Jose' she was going to have the ugly black painted over as soon as she got the Charger.

He remembered the conversation he had with Sally, "I'm sorry but I've already bought the car. I still have one payment to have enough for the down payment," she had said. "I really do need a car that doesn't break down every day. That Volvo is in the shop more than it on the road. The mechanic told me it had died several months ago but no one bothered to tell it. His suggestion was to see if I could sell it for scrap."

He had told her the rent he was willing to pay would cover the down payment.

She seemed reluctant but after much persuasion she finally agreed to rent him the car for a part of a day.

"As soon as I get possession I'm going to have it repainted. If you give me the money to finish the down payment, I'll rent it to you after I have it painted." It didn't take long for Sally to make up her mind about renting out the car. She was sick of Old Ugly.

"No, no, don't do that my friend loves the metallic black."

"But that black has got to go,"

He needed the Charger before the decal was removed. And if Sally followed through afterwards with the paint job, that would be great for two reasons. The charger would no longer be black and it would no longer have the decal.

"Okay I tell you what I'll do. I'll give you the rent up front today. Then tomorrow morning I'll pick it up. Afterwards I'll deliver it to the paint shop. I'll even deliver the Volvo to Al's Junk Yard for you. It's a long way and in a bad section of town you wouldn't want to be in. It's scary out there, no place for a pretty young woman anyway."

Luther's flattery closed the deal.

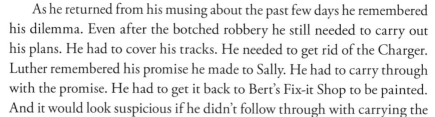

As he returned from his musing about the past few days he remembered his dilemma. Even after the botched robbery he still needed to carry out his plans. He had to cover his tracks. He needed to get rid of the Charger. Luther remembered his promise he made to Sally. He had to carry through with the promise. He had to get it back to Bert's Fix-it Shop to be painted. And it would look suspicious if he didn't follow through with carrying the Volvo to the junk yard.

"I have to get rid of the gun. Maybe I can hide the gun in the junk. There's plenty of it. The place is full of piled up junk. It's everywhere. There's hardly enough room for a skid-loader to maneuver around them."

Then he remembered his other trip there, how the scrubby old man had appeared out of nowhere. "I can't be found looking around the yard for a good place to hide a gun."

"And I have to stow the money away for a while. I can't be spending any of the money now."

With all the preparation he had put into pulling off the robbery, it never crossed his mind that things would not work out as planned. He had not thought about a plan B. So there was no plan B.

He had to keep a low profile until things settled down. But with his accidentally shooting the guard that would take a very long time.

"Now where would be a good place to hide a briefcase full of stolen money? I've heard it said 'If you want to hide something hide in plain sight.' But I can't leave it here. It's like an open house with people always coming and going."

"I have to get my head on straight. I can't let this cloud my brain. Think! Think!" he demanded of his brain. He was pacing the floor again.

"It's getting late. I have to deliver the Charger to Bert's shop to be painted. I have to carry the Volvo to Al's junkyard before they close. I can't wait around. I have to do something now!"

He went out to the Charger to get his change of clothes. When he returned home from the robbery he had grabbed the briefcase and ran into the house. When he brought in the dirty clothes he decided to put the briefcase in his clothes hamper which was already half full. He put the other dirty clothes on top.

"That will have to do until I get back," he told himself. Then he thought of the gun still in the briefcase. "I have to get rid of that gun now." He pulled the clothes back out of the hamper and lifted the briefcase out and put it on the bed to get the gun. When he opened it he noticed something was not right. All of the stacks of bills were in an orderly line except for one. It was slightly skewed.

"It must have slipped when I threw it in the trunk. I can't deal with this now," he muttered as he took the gun out and settled the lose stack back in place. He then returned the briefcase back among the dirty clothes. That's when he noticed the ball cap with his old hair glued to it. He had forgotten about in the rush to get out the back gate. He donned the long

haired cap and he dabbed the prepared paint brush on his face to make him appear to have a short beard.

He drove the Charger to Bert's and left it parked in front as he was instructed to do and got into the Volvo. As he headed to Al's Junk Yard the car began to shake. It was a rough ride to start with but it got worse as he drove. He was a few miles away when the car started making a thumping noise.

He remembered that Sally had a lot of trouble with 'Old Ugly' as she called the car. That's why it was headed to Al's to be scrapped.

"Just my luck," Luther grumbled as he continued to drive on. He hoped he could make it to Al's but the thumping got worse. He stopped and found the trouble. One of the wheels was bare. The rubber was completely gone.

"Damn," he yelled as he hit the side of the lid with his fist and kicked the bare rim. His nerves were shot from what had already happened.

The events of the day flashed through his mind as he hobbled on his injured foot and paced back and forth shaking his bruised hand.

"I didn't mean to shoot anybody. The gun just went off. The guard startled me when he rushed in."

He opened the trunk in search of a spare. It was filled with bags of trash and junk. He hauled out the bags and pushed aside the pieces of broken metal. His search produced a rusted jack and tire tools scattered on top of the spare that had been tossed in. It seemed to be on its last leg as well. "It does have a little air in it. Maybe it'll hold up until I reach the junk yard."

As he put the old rim in the trunk something flashed in his mind. His nerves had calmed somewhat and his mind seemed to be working again. The idea dawned on him and grew as he was closing the lid of the trunk. The car was going to be crushed. That would be a good way to get rid of the gun. So he put the worn out wheel rim and tire tools in the spare tire well and stowed the gun in the middle of the rim. He piled the trash bags and metal scrap on top and drove the old car to the junk yard to be crushed.

"That was a stroke of luck," he changed his mind about what luck meant. This time it was good luck.

But his good luck didn't last long. As luck would have it, the car wasn't crushed after all. Other matters took precedence. There were several stolen cars that needed to be destroyed first. So the car was stowed in the 'dead bodies' lot'. Two young men rented the 'junker', used it in a botched liquor store robbery and wrecked it when the tire blew out. The gun was found later and turned over to a forensics expert. There was also part of his makeshift wig stuck to the carpet in the trunk of the Charger. The wig he had made of his own hair.

Luther revealed the long story about the botched robbery to Kayla. "It was an accident. I didn't mean to shoot anybody," He paced nervously back and forth as he finished. "I kept watching the news. I knew it wouldn't be long before they found out I was the one who pulled the robbery not Danny. That's why I needed to get away. When I saw that policeman headed right toward me, I was sure he was going to arrest me. It would all be over then. When he yelled for me to stop I panicked and ran."

They sat in silence as the sun began to peek over the horizon. Kayla didn't know what to say. The young man was in deep trouble. What could she say to help? What happened was his fault. He chose to rob the company. He chose to carry the loaded gun. She believed him when he said it was an accident. But it was his decision to carry a loaded gun. Yet she felt compelled to help him.

"So now that you know what I've done, do you think your God will help me?"

"I'm sure of it but it may not be the way you want. As I said I don't pretend to know all the answers, far from it. I know God forgives our sins but we have to repent and ask for that forgiveness. However we still have to suffer the consequences of wrong doing. Our laws exact punishment for crimes. You did rob which is against the law. And our laws are based on God's laws so I don't know what God would expect of you. Let's pray about it and ask God for guidance."

During the course of the day Luther seemed interested in learning more about God and what being a Christian meant.

After Kayla explained the plan of salvation to Luther, he decided it would be a good idea. "I've heard that judges give lighter sentences to people who become a Christian."

"You can't accept Christ just to escape prison. It doesn't work that way. Accepting Christ means you turn your life completely around. You repent of your sins, ask for forgiveness, and promise to follow Him, to do His will not your own. Your life is totally changed. It's all or nothing. What you thought was important is no longer so. Besides that judges aren't fooled that easily. They just might take offence at the attempt and it could make things a lot worse.

CHAPTER 23

STILL MISSING

"It's like they dropped off the face of the earth. We have an APB out for Kayla's car but no one has heard or seen anything. What's with this woman? She keeps showing up on our radar," Sheriff Hayes asked Erica. "You did the work-up on her. Is there anything you learned in your investigation that will help in the search?"

"Nothing comes to mind. Her record is clean. There is no reason for her to flee as Mrs. Latimore suggested, since Judge Lawson granted her temporary custody of Sandy."

"Her neighbor seems to think she went on a trip because she saw her put something large in her trunk. She said it could have been luggage. According to her they were dressed in shorts and tees. Evidently the lady doesn't have much to do since she keeps close watch on the neighborhood. We found only one thing that raised a red flag. She left her purse and cell phone in her bedroom. That's not much to go on. But a woman wouldn't go on a trip without her purse. There's little we can do since she isn't officially missing. So Erica, since you did all the leg work on Kayla would you mind following up on this to see what you can find?"

"I'd be happy to. I've already checked hotels. There's no record of her checking into one within seven hundred miles. She grew up in an orphanage so I don't think she has any relatives to visit. Maybe I should take a closer look in her house to see if anything is amiss. But how would I know?"

"I need to get back with the city precincts and work on the construction murder-robbery. It's so confusing. Danny insists that he had nothing to do with it. He still swears the fifty-dollar bill from the robbery floated down and landed at his feet. I am not yet convinced he's guilty of that crime. Oh I think he's guilty alright but I don't know what he's guilty of."

Erica called Talitha to meet her at Kayla's. "Since you have a key I won't be breaking and entering," she explained, "besides I know nothing about Kayla's home and wouldn't know if anything was out of order. Since you two are such good friends I assumed you would know if something was out of kilter."

"The sheriff is right Kayla wouldn't go on a trip without her purse. He said the woman next door saw her putting something in the trunk. She thought they were suitcases. But her luggage is still here and most of her clothes are still in the closet. So that theory is ruled out," Talitha commented as she checked around the bedroom. "Kayla always keeps an orderly house and I don't see anything out of place in here."

"Let's try the kitchen. We stocked up on snacks and food a child would eat when we went to the grocery. I don't see much left. But one never knows how long the supply will last with a child around. Kayla isn't used to having a child to feed. Maybe she just needed to replenish her larder. In that case she wouldn't need a purse. It would be just one more thing to carry. All she would need would be: money, car keys, and driver's license. There's nothing unusual on her shopping list she keeps on the refrigerator."

"Okay what are we overlooking? Let's go back over what we know." Erica's analytical training kicked in, "Kayla and Sandy are not here. Her car is not here. But her purse and cell phone, items most women take with them, are here. There is no evidence that anything unusual happened here at her house. Everything seems to be in order."

"Alright," Talitha followed Erica's example as she mentally backed off and tried to see things from another perspective. "If there was an emergency Kayla would have grabbed her purse, which held her keys, driver's license, and phone and rushed out the door. If she went grocery shopping, she would have grabbed her purse, etcetera, the grocery list from the refrigerator and rushed out the door. The list is still on the refrigerator so that's out."

"And her car is gone," Talitha rushed back to the bedroom and picked up Kayla's purse and searched the pockets for car keys. "What was I thinking? Of course they're not here. Her car isn't here." She looked for the case that held her credit cards. It was still in the purse. "Her driver's license and change purse are not in her purse. She wasn't going to buy much if she went shopping because she didn't carry her credit cards. So if my theory is right she was just going to make a short trip to pick up a few things."

"The last day her neighbor saw her was several days before Saturday. That could mean she has been gone maybe four days. I don't think she would have left her purse and cell phone if she planned to be gone that long. Something must have happened; but what?" Erica wondered aloud as they were on the way out.

As Talitha took her spare key out to lock the door, she noticed a letter sticking out of the mailbox. "Oh! Her mail! I haven't thought of that. I wonder how long it's been since she checked it. This should give us some idea how long she's been gone." She reached out and raised the lid. "The box is full. The neighbor must be right. It's been several days. Now I'm really worried. Do you think the extortionist could have something to do with it?"

"If that's the case it must have happened after she left the house since nothing is amiss here. Maybe she was being watched."

The search for Kayla's car had been extended to include several states but there had not been any leads that panned out.

While Erica, Talitha, and Gabe were concentrating on finding Kayla most of the other police were working on the construction company case. The investigation seemed to be at a standstill; all the leads were becoming stale.

"Since some of these crimes seem to be related I think we need put them together and see what we have," Sheriff Hayes wheeled out a large white board where he had written down a list facts on one side. Then he sketched a map of the city and wrote the names of places involved in each case. Beside each location he wrote the names of the people and the two cars involved. Because there were so many places that would have more than one name or car he decided to use colored pens and draw lines to the different locations. By the time he was through the board was a mishmash of colored lines. "Well so much for that plan," He erased the board and wheeled it away.

"Sheriff you had the right idea but there was too much on one page. Why don't we try the same approach in a different format?" Rebeca suggested. "Mike Core's been itching to get in on the construction case why don't we take him up on it. He's good with computers. We could use a city map then develop other pages using only one person per page. Then overlap a page at a time."

The process led to one conclusion. They needed to concentrate on the mystery man who rented the Charger from Sally. He must have been the one who drove it to the construction company. Everything seemed to revolve around Danny, Sally, two cars, and the mystery man.

"I think we need to question Danny again," Chief White decided. "He's our best lead so far but I don't think he is our mystery man. It doesn't make any sense. He knows Sally and wouldn't call her to rent the Charger. He'd just ask to use it."

"And the hair sample found in the Charger did not match his DNA," the sheriff added.

The discussion continued as each officer pointed out item after item from the composite.

"He does not match the description Joe gave. But he is our only suspect."

"He did have the fifty-dollar bill from the robbery."

"The gun was found in the Volvo that was registered to him."

"Since Sally was his friend he did have access to the Charger."

"Here's another piece of the puzzle that doesn't seem to match the picture. And I think you'll find it interesting." Erica told the group as she entered the station carrying a long plastic box.

"We found this under Danny's bed. It contains pictures of Kayla. There are also newspaper clippings, and notes all pertaining to Kayla.

"Now that puts another wrinkle in the picture. The puzzle we're working on has too many extra pieces. We have Danny tied the murder case but he seems to have something to do with Kayla. And Kayla is missing along with Sandy.

Danny had been questioned for over an hour and they were still not sure he was guilty of the murder. He was given just enough information about of their findings to give him a good scare. He tried to explain away the circumstances he found himself in. When they mentioned the murder weapon he became terrified. He was guilty of a lot of crimes but murder wasn't one of them. This whole affair had turned against him. Could he be facing the death penalty?

Erica was sent in to continue the questioning. She carried in the box and slammed it on the table in front of Danny. He was stunned when he saw it was his box she had brought in with her.

Before he had time to compose himself, Erica placed her hands on the table as she leaned in toward him with fire in her eyes, "Where is Kayla and Sandy? What have you done to them?" The blunt questions were intended to shock him into confessing.

It worked. Danny found himself in danger of having multiple murder charges brought against him.

"I have no idea where they are. I'm just as surprised as you are. I haven't done anything to them." He tried to keep his composure as he answered the questions Erica asked.

"Yes, he had asked Sally to watch Kayla. Yes, He had compiled a dossier on Kayla. And yes, he was the extortionist.

"But I tell you I have no idea where they are." He pleaded for her to believe him. "And I had nothing whatsoever to do with the murder of that security guard."

Danny was somewhat relieved to get it off his chest as he confessed to his treachery. Sandy had been raised by her great grandmother. He was her only living relative after her great grandmother, his grandmother, died. That's when he hatched up the idea to collect ransom by using his cousin as a pawn. His scheme had gotten out of control. But he was not a murderer.

Multiple charges were brought against him including extortion, child endangerment, and child abuse. He was not aware the officers really didn't think he was the murderer. But he was still not off the hook. He was their only suspect.

Chapter 24

KAYLA'S INJURED

"No Sandy, come back," Kayla shouted as she ran after the child who was trying to catch a rabbit that had scampered underneath a bush.

It had been a long sleepless night for Kayla and Luther as shared each other's plight. But Sandy was awake and ready to run and play. The rabbit was standing on its hind legs looking around when Sandy spied it and started the chase. It darted in and out of the bushes with Sandy in pursuit. Kayla ran after them as they headed toward the stacks of debris at the edge of the yard. That's where Luther had piled the brush, trash, and broken playground equipment when he cleared a place for Sandy to play.

As they neared the perimeter of the yard Kayla dashed after them in fear Sandy would go into the overgrown thicket. Her foot snagged on a vine which sent Kayla plunging into the pile of rubble. Luther caught Sandy and carrying her under his arm and went back to check on Kayla. He was shocked. She was impaled in her side by an old spike.

"NO! Don't pull it out yet," Kayla cautioned.

Luther was beside himself with fear and uncertainty. He was still holding Sandy as he kneeled beside her. When he saw the blood trickle down, he panicked, "Oh God! Oh God!"

The image of his mother lying in a pool of blood flashed across his eyes. He had slipped from his hiding place from under the old stairs. His father had stopped yelling for him and stumbled to the bedroom in a drunken stupor.

Kayla saw he was hyperventilating. "Luther I need your help," she told him in a quiet voice. She had to keep talking or he might lose focus again.

"Put Sandy in the building with her backpack. Then get a sheet from the pantry-storage room, tear it into strips."

Kayla kept giving him directions in a calm voice, "You have to be quick when you pull the rod out. Put towels over the hole and press hard. *"And I'll try not to faint."*

When she woke up she noticed Luther had tied the strips of cloth around her. He lifted her arm and put it around his neck and grabbed her around the waist trying not to disturb the bulky bandage. She could barely walk as he helped her to the building. She had passed out again by the time he eased her onto the mattress on the floor.

"The spike went all the way through. She's in bad shape. She could bleed to death if she doesn't get to a hospital. If I take her there I'll be arrested. But if she dies I would be responsible for two deaths. Then I'll be charged with two murders and kidnapping. I'll be put to death for sure." He was pacing outside trying to decide what to do. His thoughts were all in a jumble. *"I can't think straight with her in there bleeding to death."*

He panicked and automatically as if by rote headed for the car.

Kayla had seen the fear and uncertainty in Luther's eyes. She could tell he was petrified. He was going to leave her there. She could die if he left. She wasn't going to let Sandy witness that.

"Sandy, don't cry. Mommy's okay. But you need to listen carefully to Mommy. Okay?'

"Okay," Sandy sniffled.

Kayla punched a hole in her driver's license. She took a drawstring from the backpack and threaded it through the hole and put it around Sandy's neck.

She told Sandy to get some snacks and water and put them in the backpack. "Now put it in the car on the floor of back seat. Then we'll play hide and seek. Before Mr. Man comes back you go hide in the car with your backpack."

"Can you remember to do that?"

"Okay, I'll hide real good so Mr. Man can't find me."

"Mommy may pretend to take a nap. Give me a goodnight kiss." She knew she might pass out.

"Lord Jesus, take care of Sandy," she prayed, "And I need your healing hand."

Luther was not aware of the child sleeping in the floorboard. He exited the interstate and took backroads as he searched for a way to get rid of Kayla's car. He was sure the police had an APB out for it by now. When he came to a small town he looked for an opportunity to abandon the car. He pulled beside a used car lot then noticed it had too the security cameras. He tried to swap cars at several other places but nothing worked. He had been on the road for hours and was getting low on gas.

He pulled up to the convenience store gas pump and went in to pay. Sandy got up from where she had been hiding, rubbed the sleep out of her eyes with her fists, and looked out the window. She had been lulled to sleep with the motion and whir of the car. "Mommy," she called as she looked around, "I gotta go."

No one was there to hear her so she opened the car door and started inside.

A couple exiting the store held the door open for her, "She must be with the man paying for the gas." The man commented to the woman, "I don't understand parents these days. They don't think anything about leaving a child in the car as they 'run in for just a second'. You hear warnings all the time on the news warning people to not leave children in the car."

Sandy was wandering around between the tall shelves looking for the restroom as Luther pumped the gas and left. Not finding one she went up to the counter and asked the clerk, "Where's the restroom please?" just as she had heard Kayla ask.

The clerk looked over the counter and saw the small child looking up at her.

"Where's your mommy sweetheart?" the clerk looked around and found no one.

"She's sleeping," Sandy answered.

"Is she outside? I'll go get her."

"I gotta go!" Sandy said as she pulled at her clothes and twisted around in urgency.

"I don't think much of a mother who lets her child wander into a store by herself. I'd go get her but she can't wait," Patricia mumbled to herself as she hurried Sandy to the restroom.

"Do you need help?"

"No thank you," Sandy answered as she rushed in and shut the stall door.

"Well at least she taught her good manners. But a child shouldn't be out this late. Well I may be speaking out of turn they may be on vacation. I've been known to travel late at night while on vacation. That could be the reason her clothes are dirty and stained. But why would she have dark stains on the back too?" she commented as she went out to get the mother. But there wasn't a car in sight.

"Walter, I know it's late but I need you," she called her friend at the police station.

"Wow Pat, you must really be lonesome. I'll be right there," he teased before she could explain the problem to him.

"Now Walter, don't get yourself all hot and bothered. I just need you to get over here right now. I'll explain when you get here."

When Walter walked in the door Sandy freaked out and ran to the storage room.

"I don't know if it's because you're a man or if it's your ugly face she's afraid of."

"Has she told you anything about her parents?"

"Not much. I asked her where her mother was and she said her mommy was sleeping. I went out to get her mother but there wasn't even a car out there."

"Why did she come in the store?"

"She wanted to use the restroom. I heard this small voice asking where it was. I looked down over the counter and there she was. I looked around and didn't see anyone else."

"Did you find out anything else? Why she was alone?"

"I don't know why she was alone. But there is one thing. Her clothes were dirty and had an odd smell. So I took it upon myself to change her since no one was here to protest."

"Let me see them. Sometimes we can tell a lot about a person by the type of clothes and the tags in them."

Patricia handed Walter the clothes, "They seem to be new. But you can tell she's had them on for a while."

When Walter saw the dark stains he frowned, "I think that's blood. You said she doesn't have any open wounds so the blood probably isn't hers. And that stain on the back of her shirt looks like a hand print."

"When I kept asking about her Mommy she said 'Mommy got hurt on a stick.' Maybe it's her mother's blood."

"I'm carrying her to the emergency room to get her checked out."

"Since she ran when you came in, I don't think she'll go with you. Let me call Mel to take over for me. Maybe she'll be alright if I'm with you."

"That's odd Sandy isn't afraid of Mel. She talked to him when he went back there," Patricia told Walter as she came back from the storage room.

"Let me try something,' Walter suggested as he took off his top shirt and went into the storage room and knelt in front of Sandy.

"She's fine as long as I don't have on my uniform. She's must be afraid of police."

"But how did she get here?" Patricia was still puzzled.

"Why don't we **ask her**?" Mel suggested.

"How did you get here?" Patricia asked as she took her hand and led her out of the storage room.

"In a car," was the answer.

"Oh boy, at this rate it's going to take a long time," Walter moaned.

"Did your mommy bring you here?" Patricia tried another approach.

"No."

"Let's try a different tactic." Mel sat her in a chair and squatted in front of her at eye level. "What's your name?"

"Sandy Adair."

Walter went outside and called his station, "Check to see if there's an alert for a lost child named Sandy Dare. If there isn't one put one out. She's here with me now."

"I was so worried about finding her mother, asking her name didn't even cross my mind." Patricia was appalled at herself. That should have been the first thing she asked.

"Okay Sandy can you tell me how your mommy got hurt with a stick?" Mel asked.

That's when Sandy started talking. She told them all about trying to catch the rabbit hopping around in the yard. It took a long time before she got to the point where her mother fell on a stick and took a nap. When she wound down they still didn't know much. So they decided to give the questioning a rest.

"She's probably hungry and thirsty," Mel suggested as he reached for a pack of crackers and took a half pint of milk from the cooler.

"Mommy fixed a picnic for me but I left my pack in the car," she told Mel as she snacked.

"Did your mommy put the picnic in your pack?"

"Yes she took the string and out of it and the water kept falling out." Sandy answered as she swung her feet back and forth and looked around.

"You have to be patient and let children answer their way. They tell you a lot if you listen carefully." Mel explained. "They remember things that are important to them. For example, the string from her back pack and the water falling out means something to her. The snacks I gave her made her think of the picnic she left in the car."

"Did your mommy go on the picnic with you?"

"No, she said she was going to take a nap. Mommy's funny she doesn't take naps." Sandy jumped down from the chair and wandered around the store calling an end to the conversation.

"How do you know so much about children?" Pat asked.

"I have two of my own."

"You surprise me, Mel."

"Why? Because I have children?"

"No because you're smarter than you look. Which doesn't really say much," she laughed.

"Well I've learned from my own two you have to let them talk. You'd be surprised at the information they give you. It's like a scavenger hunt. You have to pay attention, look for clues, and then assemble the facts."

When they pulled into the hospital parking lot Sandy began to protest, "No, No, No I don't like this place!"

"Okay we know two things about her. She's afraid of police and hospitals."

"Let's go wake up Doc. He may be a little grumpy for waking him up at five o'clock but maybe he'll check her out."

He came to the door in his robe. Sandy was fine until he started to put on his white scrubs. That's when she froze.

"So we now we know she's also afraid of doctors."

"She seems to be fine except for this rash on her chest," the doctor said as he rubbed lotion between his hands to warm it before he patted it on the rash.

"I noticed the rash when I changed Sandy's clothes. A makeshift necklace was the culprit. She said it itched her." Patricia relayed to them the conversation she had with Sandy about the necklace.

She failed to mention the rest of what Sandy said, "Mommy told me not to take it off. And we played hide and seek with Mr. Man."

Patricia mumbled to herself. "Why would anyone use an old driver's license as a necklace anyway? I guess she was copying the idea of dog tags from the military."

"What driver's license?" Walter had heard the mumble.

"It was scratching her chest. So I took it off when I took off her shirt."

"What driver's license?" Walter asked again.

"And I put one of the shirts from the store on her.' she continued. "Do you think the owner will mind? Well if he does I'll just pay for it myself."

"**What driver's license**?" he asked again in a loud agitated voice.

"That's what I'm trying to tell you. It was scratching the child so I threw it away."

"**What?**"

"Trash was picked up thirty minutes ago," Mel answered the frantic call from Walter. But I think we need to find Sandy's mother fast if it's not already too late. I was going over what Sandy told us and came to this conclusion. If her mother does not take naps and she kept napping after she got hurt, she must be in shock from the trauma."

They were at a loss. Some woman was in desperate need of their help. She was somewhere out there probably at the point at death and they had no clue how to find her. The only link was this precious child. There had been no response from the alert they put out for Sandy Dare.

Chapter 25

SANDY FOUND SAFE

Walter's anxious call about trash pickup made Mel go back and check again to make sure the trash was gone. That's when he found the small bag containing Sandy's clothes behind the dumpster. Apparently it had fallen out as Pat threw the bags in it. Kayla's driver's license in the bag gave them enough information for Walter to start a search. It listed Live Oak as her address. That's when they found that Sandy Adair not Sandy Dare was on the missing person's alert system. The authorities in Oasis notified the Sheriff in Live Oak to let him know they had found Sandy.

Gabe had badgered the police department with constant calls for any news from Kayla. He was frantic with worry and felt so helpless. "It's been days since the drag net for Kayla's car has been out. How could it evade detection so long?" Gabe wanted to know.

Talitha too had been persistent in calling for any news about Sandy and Kayla. Erica understood how frustrated they were. She promised them she and the entire force were doing everything in their power to find them. She also promised they would let them as soon as any news came. So Erica kept the promise. As soon as the police in Oasis called she contacted them.

"Talitha, Sandy's been found. She's okay." Erica called with the good news.

"Thank you Lord," Talitha was so relieved, "How did they find her?"

"We got a call from the Oasis police station fifteen hundred miles from here. Sandy is okay but Kayla isn't with her. They don't know where Kayla is. Sandy was alone when she was found in a convenience store. They have no idea how she got there. She had Kayla's driver's license. It listed Live Oak as her residence. The information was enough for the authorities in Oasis to contact us here in Live Oak."

She didn't tell her they had found the license on a string around Sandy's neck. She knew Kayla would not have punched a hole in her driver's license unless it was a dire emergency. *"She sure is one smart woman."* Nor did she tell her Kayla may be injured. *"There's no need to get everyone upset until we know for sure."*

When Erica called Gabe and relayed the same information, Gabe instantly caught on the words 'Kayla's license'. That made him more alarmed. Kayla would not have given them to Sandy unless there was a very good reason. He felt so helpless. She was out there somewhere possibly in great danger and he couldn't do anything. But he could. He was going to Oasis. He rushed to find Erica for more information about where Sandy was found, but he met a throng of people there. The news was already out.

"Nathanael sure works fast," he muttered as he elbowed his way through ignoring the stares and nasty comments.

Talitha and Nathanael were also part of the crowd at the police station. They had rushed there to learn more but they found themselves surrounded by others who wanted news as well. They were shocked when they learned Sandy had been found so far away.

It was a din of noise as they all talked at the same time. It seemed the entire town was out in front of the courthouse or at the Daily News hammering for some information about Sandy and Kayla. They were distraught that Kayla was still missing. There were so many unanswered questions. Where did they find Sandy? Was she all right? Where was Kayla? Why wasn't she with Sandy? How did Sandy get that far from home?

Nathanael was bewildered. "We've been broadcasting the missing persons' search for days. I don't know how that slipped through the net,"

The authorities in both cities were undecided about sending Sandy home to Live Oak. They thought it might be best for her to stay in Oasis. It was a possibility she could help locate Kayla if she stayed. She may be able to shed some light on where she might be. Communication between the two stations was constant. Back in Oasis they were learning a little at a time from Sandy. Mel was very helpful. He was able to decipher a lot as he talked with Sandy. Kayla had told her to hide in her car. She was playing hide and seek with Mr. Man. That's why she was in Kayla's car. It worried them that Kayla didn't go with her and Mr. Man because she was taking a nap after getting hurt with a stick. Then there was the bloody hand print on Sandy's clothes. But they kept these last two facts out of the news.

As soon as Talitha found out they were keeping Sandy in Oasis she headed for the airport. She went to the information desk to check for an airline that would have a direct flight to the airport close to Oasis. She was going to catch the next flight out to Oasis even if she had to bribe another passenger to give up his or her seat. When she got to the information desk there was Nathanael leaning against a wall grinning at her.

"I thought I'd find you here," he said as he pushed away from the wall and headed her way. "Yep, I thought you'd show up too," he turned and spoke to Gabe who just as showed up as well. "Come on I've got a jet fueled up, preflight checked, flight plans logged, and ready to go. By the time you get a ticket and go through the boarding process we can already be half way there. Besides the nearest international airport is seventy miles from Oasis. There's an airport closer that can accommodate my plane. I have a rental car already scheduled for pickup."

"I'm almost ready to change my mind about you. You noticed I did say almost. Man you sure work fast." Gabe said as he buckled himself in the copilot's seat. He couldn't express how thankful he was.

"We have people as the old saying goes. Some do nothing but schedule and arrange."

I'm in trouble there's no way I can compete with this man. I'm way out of his league but I'll do anything to find Kayla. I'll even put up with this news hound.

Talitha was thinking along the same lines, *I'm aware that Nathanael may be after a big story but I'm willing to take him up on this flight to be able to get to Sandy and find Kayla.*

Sandy ran to Talitha as soon as she spied her. She reached for Gabe as well. She even greeted Nathanael. The three had flown to Oasis to be with Sandy while they searched for Kayla. They met at Mel's house where Sandy was staying. Mel was able to get information from her a little at a time. Because of this she was allowed to stay with Mel and his family. His two girls and Sandy hit it off at once.

Talitha and Sandy pulled into a shopping center to shop for clothes when Sandy stopped short and pointed at a man loading a piece of farm equipment. He was wearing well-worn jeans and tee shirt. An old well-used ball cap covered part of his long hair.

"Mr. Man," she called.

The man turned and smiled.

"Oh he's not Mr. Man." The smile on her face fell.

"Who is Mr. Man?" Talitha asked.

"He drove Mommy's car a long ride. He helped her walk when she fell. He made Mommy stop sweeping when it made me sneeze."

Talitha texted Erica with the information Sandy had given her. She described the man Sandy had called Mr. Man.

"That's the same description of our mystery man!"

Erica rushed in to tell her chief, "Get out the construction murder file Chief. I think I have a lead."

She didn't wait when the chief pulled out the files. She grabbed the folder and thumbed through until she found what she was looking for.

"Here it is. The man Joe said helped him sell the car. His name was, Luther. He had a long light brown beard and mustache and always wore an old beat-up ball cap over long unkempt hair. That fits the description of the man Sandy was with. Talitha gave the same description of a man Sandy thought was Mr. Man."

"That's Luther," Jose' gasped. He was watching the news when he saw the composite of the mystery man. He kept hearing news about a car that may have been used in the robbery-murder and thought no more of it until it finally dawned on him. The car was a Charger. **He** was the Joe they were searching for. They wanted to bring him in 'for questioning'. He was in danger of being arrested because he didn't come forward sooner. But he didn't realize Luther was the mystery man they were searching for. He knew Luther. He wasn't a killer. He wasn't what you call a loner. But he didn't have close friends. He was friendly enough and could strike up a conversation with just about anyone. He was one of those people who could hold up his end of a conversation but most often he was not the one doing the talking. He was a good listener. He just didn't trust people. There must be some mistake. Luther may be a small time crook but he wasn't a killer. That's why he didn't know **he** was the **Joe** they were looking for. But they may not take his word for it. He had heard that 'ignorance of the law was no excuse'.

Chapter 26

LUTHER RUNNING SCARED

"Howard the Coward, go ahead hit me you coward. You've been thinking of it for years," his father's voice kept hounding him. "You'll never amount to anything." That was the last thing his father had said to him. He had stepped between his father and mother. He tried to protect his mother from his father's rage but couldn't. His father had grabbed him by the front of his shirt and flung him against the wall as if he were a rag doll. He at fourteen had outgrown his hiding place under the old stairs. He was no longer a terrified child. But he was not yet a man strong enough to stand up against his father. He felt helpless not being able to help his mother. He just couldn't tolerate the abuse any more. So he ran.

It seemed he had been running all his life. Living on the streets taught him to escape when he had the chance. And here he was running away again. He had left a woman and child alone out in the wilderness. The woman would most likely die from her wounds. He ran when he shot the guard. His father may have been right about him; he was a coward. He changed his name to Luther because of his fathers' taunt, 'Howard the Coward'. He hated the name Howard.

He was still driving Kayla's car but he had no desire to steal another one. He was sick at heart. Nothing mattered anymore. Then he thought of what his future might be. He could look forward to being holed up in a dark cell waiting for the death chamber.

It made him remember how scared he was as he hid in the dark space under the stairs. It had been a safe place because his father didn't know about it. But it was a dark scary place. He could hear his mother's screams.

While he waited there for the carnage to stop his thoughts turned to the horrors of death. These thoughts would haunt him for days.

The sound of the wheels turning on the highway began to taunt him like his father had so many years ago. Howard the coward, Howard the coward, Howard the coward kept time with the wheels. He had left his mother in a pool of blood. Now he had left another helpless woman to die. He was a coward. He wasn't a bully like his father but he was not much better. Much to his horror he was following in his father's footsteps. He would go to jail for murder just as his father had. But unlike his father he would not be released after serving a few years. It would be much worse for him. He had killed a guard. It was the same as killing a policeman. If Kayla died that would be two deaths on his record. He would get the death sentence for sure.

Luther pulled off on a side road. He couldn't stand the taunting wheels any longer. He leaned his head against the steering wheel. He was tired and weary. His mind wouldn't let him rest. He was a small child again helplessly hiding from the world in the dark hole. It was hard to breathe in the small dank chamber. He peeked out through a crack and saw images of his mother and Kayla covered in blood swirling around. He wanted to call out to his mother but knew if he did so his father would find him. The two bloody women were calling to him for help. The vision terrified him. But he couldn't help them; he was deathly afraid for his own safety. He was so scared and ashamed he started to cry. He pressed his hands over his mouth to stifle his screams to keep his father from hearing. But his father must have found his hiding place. He was banging on the boards.

He woke gasping for breath tears streaming down his face. Someone was rapping on his window. "Do you need help son?" The old man asked.

Kayla felt his arms wrapped around her as he kissed the top of her head. They were sitting on the floor as she leaned back against his chest. "It's okay darling I'm here."

"Gabe," she whispered.

It hurt to talk her throat was parched. Her body ached. Then she opened her eyes. It was dark outside and she realized she was still in the old building. Her heart fell. Gabe was not there. It seemed so real, but she was alone. She kept praying as she tried to stay awake. "Keep Sandy safe. Let her be found." She had just enough strength to get a drink of water from the bottle and nibble on the energy bar she asked Sandy to bring to her before she sent her to hide in the car. She knew she was in bad shape because it made her nauseous when she tried to sit up.

"Gabe," she whispered softly as a tear rolled down her cheek. "I can't do this." She scolded herself. "I can't give up."

"She needs me Lord. I can't lose hope that someone will find my driver's license." She knew there was no way she could walk out of there. It would be a long trek for someone who was perfectly healthy. And she was far from that.

"Even if they find my license how are they going to find me out here in the middle of nowhere?" She tried to move her arms and legs to keep the blood circulating but they were so heavy it was hard to lift them. She needed to keep up her strength. But she had to stop she was just making herself dizzy.

"I'm not ready to give up Lord. You're my only hope. I'm trusting on You to help me out of this dilemma I find myself in," Kayla prayed before she passed out again.

The old man had found Luther slumped over the steering wheel in dire distress. "Looks like you could use a cup of coffee," he said as he took him by the arm and ushered him out of the car and led the way to a small house.

Luther was in a bad way. He was in such a state of mind when he started talking he couldn't stop. The heavy weight of guilt he carried compelled him to continue to tell the old man about leaving a wounded woman and a small child in the old camp.

As soon as he heard this, the old man convinced him he had to call 911 immediately and let someone know where to find them back in Mesa Verde. "You don't want to have this hanging over your head all your life," the old man said as they traveled the short trip to Fair Haven.

After he made the call a huge burden had been lifted. But that wasn't the end of it. He was in big trouble and he knew it.

Luther went back to the old man's house where they talked all night. The old man listened as Luther poured out his soul. In his ramblings he told his life story. By dawn he was exhausted and spent. As he leaned forward and rested his head on his arms on the kitchen table, the last thing he heard was, "You need to put this in the hands of our Father in heaven, my son."

"It looks like we're too late. You may as well call the coroner. She'd gone." The paramedic commented as he covered Kayla with a sheet.

An anonymous tip had alerted them about the emergency in Mesa Verde. The call came from a small town four hundred miles away. The caller told them a woman's life may be at stake. He had given enough information for police to find the location of the old youth camp.

"But shouldn't we at least try to resuscitate?" Pete was second in command and shouldn't question his superior. But He had taken the job to help save lives and didn't like to give up so easily.

"You won't last long as a paramedic if you let this job get to you. You have to remember there will always be some we can't save. Why don't you finish up here while I go outside to make the call?"

"It's stifling in this old building," Bozeman said as he headed toward a tree. It was cooler under the shade.

Pete was not satisfied with Bozeman's pronouncement. He pulled the sheet back and took out the CPR equipment and began to work on his patient.

"They're on their way," Bozeman entered the building and saw what Pete was doing. "Pete, you can't bring back the dead. You have to stop beating yourself up every time we lose one." He placed a sympathizing hand on his shoulder.

CHAPTER 27

KAYLA'S CAR FOUND

Luther was still groggy when he woke up. He didn't remember going to bed. He stumbled out of bed and looked around at the strange place. He wandered out into the hallway and discovered he was in a hotel. He smelled coffee. He sure could use a cup. He was confused and still suffering the effects of the long night of revelations. He had gone back to the old man's house and they talked all night. But he had no idea how he got to this hotel. He looked down at the rumpled clothes he had slept in. "I know I look a sight but I need coffee."

The attendant was clearing away breakfast and cleaning the tables when Luther wobbled in. He was weak kneed and still unsteady on his feet. "I guess I missed breakfast, any coffee left?"

She took one look at the disheveled man and decided against clearing the food away. She could wait a little longer. Her family may need her at home but this man probably needed to eat. "Coffee's over there and breakfast is still on the bar. Help yourself. Take your time." She answered, "I'll just clean the other section."

"I didn't notice Fair Haven was this big when I came in yesterday evening," He commented as he tried to force down a few bites, *"And I didn't see this hotel either."*

"Fair Haven?"

"This is Fair Haven isn't it?"

"Well, no," she answered as she continued to clean a table in the far corner.

"What town is this? I came in late last night and didn't notice. *It must have been late since I don't remember it."*

171

She stopped her cleaning and walked over to him. It was clearly evident he needed a friend to talk to or at least a listening ear. "This is Middleton. You said you went to Fair Haven yesterday? I've never heard of Fair Haven. Are you sure that was the name?"

"Yes, I'm sure. I needed to make a phone call. I lost my cell phone and the old man didn't have one. We drove here, *at least I thought it was here*, to make an emergency call at Fair Haven Café. It was only about fifteen minutes from his house. It must be nearby." Luther didn't know why he was telling her this, but he wanted to know how he got to Middleton. "I guess I took a wrong turn as I came in last night."

This piqued her interest so she pulled out a chair and sat down. "I'm just curious, who is this old man?" she asked.

"Actually he didn't tell me his name. He's the old man who lives next to the little white church on Fair Haven Drive."

"I've lived in this area all my life and I've never heard of a place as you describe."

Luther was surprised, "Why, it's the main street leading into town. The church is just two miles down the road."

She shrugged her shoulders and went back to her cleaning.

Luther was beginning to get exasperated. He turned in his chair and faced her, "I tell you there was a road leading to this small one room white church with a beautiful tall steeple. There was a cottage next to it where an old man lived. We drove to the town of Fair Haven and used the telephone at Fair Haven café. I called the police station in Mesa Verde to tell them how to find a woman and her child. The next morning he cooked us a breakfast of ham and eggs with homemade biscuits."

The attendant was still intrigued and called the station at Mesa Verde to check it out. At least that part of his story was true. A woman had been found at an old youth camp.

"I was told a woman was found. Police, EMS, and coroner were dispatched to the scene. But there was no mention of a child. Are you all right?" she asked as his face paled.

Luther was frantic, "She must be there somewhere. She may be playing outside. Call them back. Have them check around. She was chasing a rabbit when Kayla got hurt. They have to find her!"

She made a return call to see if a child had been found. They had gone back and searched after she told them a man insisted they to go back to the camp and search for a child. No child was found. But they promised to continue the search.

"Oh! No! Sandy baby girl where are you?" He sat down, leaned over and buried his face in his hands. "Kayla now is the time to ask your God for help."

"This man must be crazy. He went to a non-existing town and used a phone at a non-existing café. He was directed by a non-existing old man to turn himself in for a crime he didn't mean to commit. Maybe he dreamed up the child as well."

He was disoriented when he walked outside. It didn't seem the same. He found Kayla's car in the back of the hotel and started out to find Fair Haven. He had to find the same route the old man used the day before when they came to town. *"They found Kayla but not Sandy?"* Everything was getting so confusing. The road had changed. It wasn't the same one he had traveled yesterday.

*"Oh no! She said the **coroner** had been dispatched for Kayla."* It suddenly dawned on him.

He knew she was in danger when he left her. It was his fault. Now it was too late. Luther was in a stupor as if he had been drugged. He was suffering from extreme exhaustion.

"There it is. That's the road. I've got to find the old man." He was desperate. "He'll help me find Sandy. I can't take it if another innocent child dies because of me."

His strength was gone, depleted from the lack of sleep and stress. His body shut down in forced rest as the car left the road.

"I was going in the opposite direction when I passed him. He had his turn signal on to turn left but there's no road there." The eye witness told the trooper. "Then I heard the crash."

The trooper didn't find anything to identify the wreck victim. The only clue he found was a fresh cup of coffee from a local hotel. A child's backpack, empty water and fruit drink bottles, and snack wrappers were on the back floorboard of the car.

"I'm checking out a wreck that happened just down the road. Coffee in this cup was still warm." He told the clerk as he held up the cup with the hotel logo. "I thought someone here may remember him."

The attendant had her purse slung over her shoulder walking out the door when she heard what the deputy said to the hotel clerk. "I think we need to talk." she motioned toward a chair. She told him about the odd conversation that she had with the man in question.

"I thought the man was crazy. He seemed harmless enough but appeared bewildered and confused as if he was suffering from a trauma. He thought he was in a town I've never heard of and used a phone at a non-existing café. An old man had driven him there to report a woman had been hurt and needed medical attention. Part of his story was true because I made a call for him and the woman was found where he said she would be found. But then he told me about an old man who lived around here. The old man encouraged him to turn himself in for some crime. I don't know of a man or church he talked about. He was worried about child as well. Maybe he dreamed it all up."

When she mentioned how anxious he was about a child he had left behind, the deputy's face took on a worried look.

"There was evidence that a child had been in the car. But we didn't find anyone else at the scene. *"Could the trash belong to the child he was asking about?"*

"Maybe he forgot his child was with him. That happens sometimes. *I hope he hasn't done something to the child. That could be the reason for his bizarre behavior."*

When the trooper ran a check on the car, he found it was a stolen vehicle and the owner Kayla Adair and a child were missing.

"The man's in bad shape," the doctor on the psych ward told the deputy. His injuries aren't that bad but in his frame of mind I doubt if he can answer your questions."

"What's wrong with him then?"

Hysterical amnesia is my diagnoses. Sometimes it's called fugue state. It's a type of amnesia that could be caused by many different things such as a traumatic experience."

"He was driving the stolen car that belonged to a missing woman."

"That could be the cause."

"It's imperative we to talk with him. Do you think he'll come out of it?"

"Most likely but it may be in a few hours, tomorrow, or a month from now."

"He may not be able to give us any information but a photo of him may help. I'll send it to the authorities in Live Oak. That's where the missing woman, Kayla Adair, is from."

"I hope that helps and I will get in touch with you if I he becomes lucid."

CHAPTER 28

DISCOURAGING REPORTS

Gabe was beside himself with anxiety when he was told Kayla may be hurt. He tried to concentrate on the lesson he was teaching. But he couldn't keep his mind from wandering. He felt so helpless so frustrated. She was out there somewhere hundreds of miles away. He wanted her home. He wanted her safe. He missed her terribly. They were good friend but he wanted more. He now admitted to himself. He wanted her safe in his arms. He kept going over the facts he had been told. Sandy told Mel Kayla had been hurt by a stick, blood was on her, and she kept sleeping. The blood tests from Sandy's shirt matched the samples of DNA that came from Kayla's hair brush. Even though he had been told all these facts he still believed she was alive. He felt she was alive and was not about to give up.

Erica had kept her promise to keep them informed of any information that came in about Kayla. She tried to keep her information factual and kept her opinion to herself. It would be a miracle if Kayla was alive. Now new information had just arrived. Kayla's car had been found five hundred miles from Oasis, where Sandy had been found. Erica hated to be the bearer of bad news but she promised she would let them know if any word came through. Kayla was not with her car. It didn't look good.

"Lord, give me direction, send me some sign. Help me find her," Gabe prayed.

"Kayla, send me a message. Please let me know you are safe." He tried to mentally reach out to her. *"I have this feeling that you are alive but need for me to pray for you. That's what I've been doing all this time. We all have been praying. One of my students let me know our students have been meeting*

at the flagpole every morning having silent prayer for you. You have to know Sandy is safe thanks to you. You have to hang on to your faith that God will take care of you and send you back to us."

The mug shot came in to Live Oak headquarters from Middleton. "That's the man." Erica grabbed the photo that came in. "He wrecked her car but Kayla was not with him! Where can she be?"

"That's Luther. There is no doubt now." Jose' slumped down in his chair as he stared at the TV screen.

"I know I should have come in before now. But I just couldn't believe Luther would murder somebody." He told the police chief as he led them to Luther's house. "I did drive the Charger to Fred's Auto for him. And the woman there thought I was Joe. But I didn't think much about it. Luther swore to me it was not a stolen car. Luther and I are friends but I keep my nose clean. I don't engage in illegal activity."

"He's being extradited as soon as the paperwork is finished. I hope he can clear up a lot of things when he gets here," he said as an afterthought as he and his deputies entered the house to search it. About two hours later Chief White came out with the briefcase. "He kept a clean house and we didn't find much to go on. We almost missed it until my deputy happened to dump his dirty clothes hamper." He told the others when he returned to the station with the briefcase. "We found the money."

Luther was still in the fugue state when he was transported back to Live Oak. He couldn't tell them anything. Kayla was still missing.

"The doctor said familiar surroundings may jog Luther's memory. We were hoping it would but it doesn't seem to be working," Erica reported to Gabe.

He was visiting with Sandy when Erica's call came in. Sandy began suffering terrible nightmares at the new foster home where she had been placed after she was returned to Live Oak. He and Tabitha were allowed to see her because of the trauma she suffered when she was in the first foster home. She still cried for Kayla but their visits helped.

"Are you talking about Mr. Man?" Sandy asked. She had overheard several conversations about Luther's return. "I want to see him."

That was a surprise. "Aren't you afraid of him?" Gabe asked.

"No, he made a place for me to play outside so I wouldn't have to stay in the big room that made me sneeze."

"It's worth a shot," Erica agreed when Gabe suggested the visit. "But I don't know if it will be allowed by my chief or social services."

The meeting was held in the hospital family visitation room. The windows let in the sunshine providing a pleasant setting. Luther sat in a wingback chair. Several deputies in plain clothes flanked each side.

Gabe, Talitha, and two social workers escorted Sandy in. As soon as she saw Luther she jerked her hand out of Tabitha's and bounded toward him before they could stop her.

"Sandy Girl," he choked as he reached out. "You're okay." Then he remembered; seeing Sandy brought him back.

"Kayla, Ah Kayla. I'm so sorry. I called and told them how to find you but it was too late." He moaned as he looked toward heaven."

Then he looked at the people in the room. They were just taking it in. Their hopes had turned to despair. "I told them where she was. They found her but it was too late." He remembered the coroner had been dispatched. He buried his head in his hands to hide his tears.

Gabe crumbled to the floor as the social workers grabbed Sandy and rushed away.

"Gabe!" Talitha was torn. Gabe needed her but Sandy needed her more. She left Gabe and rushed to comfort Sandy who was confused by what happened.

CHAPTER 29

KAYLA'S AUNT

Luther had not fully recovered from his incoherent state. He could not remember where he had left Kayla. Each agency at the station was in the midst of searching and backtracking trying to locate her when another wrinkle appeared.

A lawyer walked into the station and asked to speak with someone in charge of the Kayla Adair case. He had some news for her he explained. He had tried to contact her through normal means but had not been able to reach her. Then he saw Kayla's name on national news. She was involved in an odd kidnapping case in Live Oak. So he decided to go to Live Oak and talk directly with the authorities there.

Since Erica had been given the case he was directed to her office. No one wanted to tell him that his visit may be in vain. No one wanted to accept the fact. Talitha and Gabe were in Erica's office consoling each other as they searched for Kayla's last location. As Erica backtracked she found Middleton was where Luther had wrecked Kayla's car.

Erica picked up her phone to contact the deputy who found Luther just as the lawyer knocked at her door.

"Officer Key, I was told you might be able to help locate Kayla Adair."

He stopped when he saw the shocked looks on their faces. "I'm sorry to interrupt but..."

"I'm Erica. May I ask why you are looking for Miss Adair."

"I'm Mason McComber executor of her aunt's estate."

"Her aunt?" all three asked.

"I can't believe it. She didn't know the aunt she dreams about is real. She'll be so happy…" Talitha stopped as soon as the words left her mouth.

"I know, she told me stories about an aunt who came in her dreams and danced with her at the orphanage. I wish…," Gabe didn't want to say the word either. It was like not saying it kept it from being true.

"She was a dancer and traveled throughout the world with her troupe. She was in her sixties when her baby sister died leaving behind her daughter Kayla. She was spry lady, lived to be ninety-five. She loved her niece but circumstances… I can't say anything else. You know confidentiality."

There was no need to go into detail as to what happened at the orphanage. From the sad looks on their faces he knew something was wrong. He didn't say anything else. It would not change the past. It may make the present worse. Besides he was here to see Kayla. To make up for the wrong that the matron of the orphanage had done to her.

The matron was a master at manipulation. She convinced the aunt that infrequent visits, which because of her profession were few and far between, made Kayla unmanageable. Letters and money her aunt sent were never delivered. She led Kayla to believe there was no aunt it was a 'figment of her over-active imagination'. All contact was lost when Kayla left the orphanage.

"When you knocked I was calling the police station at Middleton. Kayla's car was found there. I hope they know where Kayla might be," Erica explained as she picked up the phone. You are welcome to stay to see if I have any luck."

"I'd like to speak to the officer who called us here at Live Oak about a stolen car which belonged to Kayla Adair," she requested. "I know you gave us the details of the wreck but I hoped I could speak with the deputy who answered the call. Maybe he can give us information that might not be in the files."

"We are trying to find Miss Adair." She explained the situation. "Luther, the man who was driving the car is unable to tell us where he left her. Maybe he said something to indicate where she may be."

"Our records just show she is missing. I'm sorry we don't have much more. The deputy who worked the wreck is out on a call and will get back to you as soon as he can."

When the deputy in Middleton got the call that someone wanted to talk with him about the wreck, he went back over his notes. The only thing in the report listed Kayla, the owner of the car, was from Live Oak and missing. There was nothing to indicate where she might be.

He told Erica these few facts that were in his report when he returned her call. "I'm sorry I can't be of help. The man was in no shape mentally to tell us anything. What he said didn't make any sense. The doctor promised to let me know if he became lucid. Which never happened before he was transported there to Live Oak."

That night the deputy couldn't sleep. Something kept nibbling at his brain keeping him awake. He kept going over the events of that day. It was something about the call from Live Oak. He got up and went to the kitchen to keep from disturbing his sleeping wife. He sat down at the table went over every detail he could remember about the wreck. The man was incoherent when they questioned him. A child's car seat and backpack in the back were found in the wrecked car.

Then it dawned on him. *'And a cup of hot coffee from the motel was in the cup holder.' That's it. That's what's bothering me. A woman at the hotel where he spent the night had talked with him. Maybe he told her something that will help."*

He remembered the story she told him. The man thought he was in Fair Haven a town where had used a phone at a café. He had talked about an old man who lived in a cabin near a church. But there was no place nearby that fit that description.

"I remember now, the car seat and backpack reminded me. She said he was *worried about a child."*

Early the next day the deputy went to the hotel in hopes he would find the same woman. He was in luck she was on duty. They sat down and discussed the matter. She methodically went over the events of that morning and tried to recall everything that happened. Each item she brought up the deputy had already heard. It was beginning to seem to be a labor of futility until she remembered the call to Mesa Verde.

"He was worried about a woman and child he left behind at an old youth camp. He said the old man had taken him to Fair Haven to make a call to Mesa Verde. He called to report a woman had been hurt and was in need of medical help. He asked me to call to make sure they found her.

Chapter 30

"It looks like we're too late. You may as well call the coroner. She'd gone." The paramedic commented as he covered the body with a sheet.

The anonymous emergency call from Middleton had led them to an old youth camp where they found the woman.

She heard voices but they came from far away. It was as if she were in a tunnel. Did she hear someone say she was gone? That couldn't be so she still felt pain in her side. "Help me!" she tried to speak but she was too weak; she didn't have the energy to force the words out. Then the light dimmed as something covered her nose making it difficult to breathe. "I can't breathe, I can't breathe," she tried speak and shake her head. She was frantic; she was being suffocated.

"It's stifling in this old building," Bozeman said as he headed toward a tree to call the coroner. It was cooler under the shade.

"No! I'm not dead! I can hear you. I can still feel pain so I can't be dead! Do something," she commanded. But the words never left her lips. Kayla willed her body to move, to wiggle her toes, to twitch her finger tips. She tried to flutter her eye lids. She ordered her head to shake the sheet off her face.

Pete was not satisfied with Bozeman's pronouncement. He was compelled to do something. He was not one to give up easily. He pulled the sheet back and took out the CPR equipment and began to work on his patient.

"They're on their way," Bozeman entered the building and saw what Pete was doing. "Pete, you can't bring back the dead. You have to stop beating yourself up every time we lose one."

"I thought I saw a slight twitch of her head." he answered as he continued to work."

"It's called a reflex. That happens sometimes. Okay since you've already started I'll help. It's good practice anyway."

Police, firemen, and coroner arrived at the camp just as the emergency vehicle, sirens screaming, pulled out headed toward the nearest hospital.

Kayla saw a dark shadow slide under the door and float around her room. Then her aunt started to dance with the shadow. The dancing figures were replaced by a bonfire. She was too close to the fire. It was so hot but she couldn't move away. She tried to open her eyes but the flames were so bright it hurt her eyes. A low dull hum gave her a headache. Then it got too cold she was freezing.

The med student was concerned, "She seems to be in distress thrashing about and moaning nonsensical words."

"Sometimes patients with a high fever and infection are delirious and have hallucinations. It's somewhat like DT's that alcoholics have," the doctor explained.

"Will she make it, Doctor?"

"I won't sugar coat it; she has a bad infection. I've given her antibiotics. I've stitched up her wounds. I've done everything within my power to save her. The rest is up to her and God. It'll be touch and go for a few days. It could go either way. Let's pray for her."

The student looked at the doctor as he bowed his head, "Lord You sent this woman my way; thank You for allowing me to tend her wounds. I've done my best and now I leave it into Your hands. Amen"

The doctor answered the unspoken question in the student's eyes, "If I took the credit I'd have to take the blame. I don't fool myself; I can do only so much. If I didn't leave it in God's hands, I'd never be able to do my job." He turned as he led the way toward another patient who was in need of his care.

Erica called Mesa Verde with a heavy heart to ask where Kayla's body was being held. She had asked Talitha, Gabe, and Mr. McComber the lawyer to be with her because she didn't want to be alone when she made the sad call.

"I'm so glad you called." The dispatcher at Mesa Verde answered the call from Live Oaks. "Yes, a woman was found at the old youth camp just where the anonymous caller said she would be. We didn't know who she was. Therefore we didn't know who to contact. She was in bad shape when EMS found her. It was touch and go for a while but she's holding her own now. She's been in a semiconscious state unable to tell us anything. She just keeps repeating something about a cave. We can't decipher what it means. But it seems to be very important to her."

Erica nearly fainted with elation. The four of them grabbed each other in a giant hug.

Erica told them what the dispatcher had said, "She keeps repeating the same word. It sounds like cave."

"Gabe, she's saying Gabe!" Talitha and Gabe recognized it at the same time.

"Hang on, Sweetheart. I'm on my way," Gabe promised as he raced out of the station.

"Nathanael," Gabe called. It was hard for him to control his excitement. His Kayla was still alive!

"I heard," he answered the phone before Gabe could say anything else. "I'm already on it. Meet me at the airport."

"You don't know how much I appreciate…," Gabe broke the long silence as they flew toward Mesa Verde.

"You know I'll do anything for a story," Nathanael interrupted him with the tease.

"I know you have feelings for…"

"You're right I do. But she doesn't love me. I was there when she needed someone to talk to. I can see how she looks at you. It's not 'just a friend' look either."

"I sure hope you're right. I'm …"

"Going to propose as soon as you see her."

"Hey! You want to have this conversation by yourself? You know what I'm going to say anyway." Gabe grinned.

"Fine with me, but I'll let you start. I'll finish." He laughed as he grasped Gabe on the shoulder, "And I expect to be your best man."

The tension that had held them in a grip for weeks eased up as they realized **they were on their way to get Kayla.**

Epilogue

Kayla and Sandy were allowed to visit Luther in prison. After the initial awkwardness, their conversation was a mixture of greeting and remembering.

He was so happy to see them both. Kayla had survived her wounds even though he had left her alone to die. He was thankful Sandy had been found safe. He didn't realize how much he had come to love her. She reminded him of the little girl he couldn't save. But he couldn't dwell on that subject. The guilt hurt too much. His only means of escape was to drown his thoughts and substitute them with something else. That's how he had survived most of his life.

"Why was it your car that I hijacked? I didn't know a child was in the car. I didn't intend to abduct anyone. I just needed a car. But you jumped in the car to save Sandy? That's how we ended up traveling together. They were all coincidences, or were they? I didn't know Sandy was hiding in your car when I almost ditched it for another one. What stopped me? Sandy could have died in the car. Who was that old man who helped me get the courage to make that emergency call? They found you just in time. The EMS worker had given up on you but the other refused to. Why? I almost called on God for help. Or maybe I did." Luther wanted to discuss all of this with Kayla but he was not yet ready to accept the answers.

"Time's up," the guard came over to remind them visitation time was over.

Kayla had been told she couldn't carry him anything when she visited. But since Luther showed an interest in learning more about God she promised to send him a list of Bible verses that may bring him comfort. She would also include the plan of salvation which she had already told him about while they were at the old youth camp.

Kayla smiled at Sandy as they walked out. That part of their life was over. They had a full life ahead of them.

"Let's go home to see Dad."

"Yeah." Sandy agreed as she reached out and took Kayla's hand.

Printed in the United States
By Bookmasters